KING OF THE EXILES

BOOKS IN THE ARGOSY LIBRARY:

GOLDEN RIVER: THE COMPLETE
ADVENTURES OF BEN QUORN, VOLUME 1
TALBOT MUNDY

LADY OF THE NIGHT WIND
VARICK VANARDY

KING OF THE EXILES
THOMSON BURTIS

FOR A POINT OF HONOR: THE COMPLETE
CASES OF RIORDAN, VOLUME 2
VICTOR MAXWELL

THE DARK WATERS
WILLIAM CORCORAN

MURDER WITHOUT MOTIVE: THE COMPLETE
CASES OF SHOW-ME McGEE, VOLUME 1
FREDERICK C. DAVIS

MURDER IN THE NUDIST CLUB
FRED MACISAAC

GORILLA CARGO: THE COMPLETE
ADVENTURES OF McNALLY, VOLUME 1
RICHARD WORMSER

GREEN MAMBA: THE COMPLETE
CASES OF DAFFY DILL, VOLUME 2
RICHARD B. SALE

THE SILENCER MYSTERY: THE COMPLETE
CASES OF GILLIAN HAZELTINE, VOLUME 3
GEORGE F. WORTS

THE ARGOSY LIBRARY

KING OF THE EXILES

THOMSON BURTIS

ILLUSTRATED BY
HARRY PARKHURST

COVER BY
EDGAR FRANKLIN WITTMACK

POPULAR PUBLICATIONS · 2024

© 2024 Popular Publications, an imprint of Steeger Properties, LLC

First Edition—2024

PUBLISHING HISTORY

"King of the Exiles" originally appeared in the September 10–October 10, 1929 issues of *Short Stories* magazine (Vol. 128, No. 5–Vol. 129, No. 1). Copyright © 1929 by Doubleday, Doran & Company, Inc.

ALL RIGHTS RESERVED

No part of this book may be reproduced or utilized in any form or by any means without permission in writing from the publisher.

Visit argosymagazine.com for more books like this.

KING OF THE EXILES

*A Super Bandit of the Mexican Border—
and a Finish Fight By the Air Route*

1

AS THE TRIM little two seated monoplane buzzed eastward along the Rio Grande, its pilot was gazing across a billowing sea of mesquite with a reminiscent look in his eyes. Once in a while his gaze dropped to the twisting silver ribbon a mile and a half beneath him, which was the Rio Grande. Every angle and turn in that stream brought back a memory to Ex-Lieutenant George Groody, and he knew almost to a tenth of a mile how far he was west of Laredo at any given moment.

Southward stretched the chaparral of Mexico, and, each time Groody's long, narrow, gray eyes swept its gray-green expanse, a little tingle went up and down his spine.

The summons which had caused himself and Tom Service in the back seat to make the long aerial trek from Hollywood, California, to McMullen, still more than two hundred miles away, seemed to hint at the fact that he would be somewhere down beyond the southern horizon before long.

Laredo came into sight, easily visible twenty miles away in the miraculously clear, golden air. More and more open fields ribbed the river and an occasional ranch-house or Mexican shack represented the outposts of civilization.

The rangy pilot relaxed slightly in his seat, and although his eyes occasionally swept the instrument board with the automatic instinct of the veteran flyer, he flew more or less mechanically. Now that the most familiar portion of the Border was rolling away behind the ship, a thousand memories of his army days swarmed to his mind. He had spent nearly three years, off and on, during the days when he had been Lieutenant George Groody, flying that same strip of tempestuous country as part of the Army Air Service Border Patrol.

He had dropped in at all the stations on his way east

for gas and oil—Yuma, Nogales, Marfa, Sanderson, Del Rio—and almost every one of them had brought back some happening of which the memory was to be cherished, now that it was a thing of the past, but which, during the actual experience, had often been a long drawn-out ordeal.

At that, though, he reflected, as he throttled the radial motor slightly and sent his ship into a gradual dive, those had been care-free days. A great deal of water had flown over the dam since he had left the army flat at the summons of the chunky man in the back seat, and, now that there was a brief respite in a continuous series of financial and other crises, Groody found that life had more flavor than it had had for a long time.

Part of the reason why he felt that his blood was flowing more swiftly through his veins at the moment was in the very vagueness of the summons which had brought him, at government expense, nearly two thousand miles. The letter he had in his pocket, with the single name "Graves" at the bottom of it, seemed to hint at vast and curiously alluring possibilities.

HE HAD PICKED out the flat, sandy airdrome of the Laredo flight now and he pulled the throttle back until the tachometer registered eight hundred revolutions as he steepened the dive. One DeHaviland was idling on the line, he noticed. Then his eyes shifted to the town. Each narrow, crooked street was familiar to him, and across the river Nuevo Laredo was a little section of the world which he never could forget. It had been his custom for years to celebrate St. Patrick's Day in a wet country, and full many a time and oft that annual celebration had taken place in the Mexican town with unique and extraordinary consequences.

Below his goggles his nose swept forward in a bold curve above a wide mouth which had a perennial droop at the right-hand corner. As though to record the fact that that slight, semi-whimsical droop was a permanent feature of his countenance, the line at that side from nostril to the corner of his mouth, abandoned a straight course and swept widely his cheek. On the other side the corresponding line was almost straight.

Many thousands of hours in the air had tanned his skin to a sort of golden mahogany hue, but beneath the tan there was a touch of red which showed through and indicated glowing health which had not always been his in the last two years. His cheekbones were high and the cheeks below lean and a trifle drawn. In his close-fitting leather helmet, he looked like some brooding eagle, as with head over the side of the cockpit, he spiraled his ship down for the landing.

He glanced at his wrist watch. Twelve-thirty. They'd have lunch in the mess hall at Laredo and make McMullen by three-thirty, if nothing happened.

He landed from the north, and tailskid and wheels touched the sand as lightly as a feather. The ship had barely hit the ground before he was turning it toward the line.

Before it had stopped rolling, fifteen feet from the DeHaviland which was warming on the blocks, he had inserted an extremely long, very thin and exceedingly black cigar in the right hand corner of his mouth. No one else in the world, as far as his friends had been able to observe, ever smoked one of those cigars, and Groody had never been so broke—which at times was very broke indeed—that he had not had a continuous supply of the specially constructed weeds being sent to him from Key West.

He ran out the motor as mechanics came toward him and his eyes rested briefly on a very small officer who was coming out from the shade of a hangar.

"It's 'Penoch' O'Reilly," he thought. "Must have landed here on patrol."

"Well," he said aloud, turning to his passenger, "last stop. This plane runs express from Laredo to McMullen."

THE ROUND-FACED MAN in the back seat took off his helmet and goggles, exposing a stiff, blond, pompadour and a pair of owlish, blue eyes. He adjusted a pair of horn-rimmed spectacles on his short nose.

"I—I crave food," he stated, and the slight hesitancy in his speech made him seem even more vague and vacuous than he appeared. "F-furthermore, I don't care if I don't f-fly again forever. M-my ears are giving out on me."

"It has been a long grind," nodded Groody, as he hopped out of the cockpit.

He was slightly over six feet tall and a considerable percentage of that altitude was devoted to legs. He was rangy and loose-jointed, but his movements had a sort of effortless sureness about them which explained various physical abilities which were his. Among them, for instance, the fact that he was alive after many years of flying, two of which had been devoted almost exclusively to being a stunt man. Groody had changed from one ship to another in the air more times than some flyers had taken off and landed.

"Hello, O'Reilly," he called to the little officer who had stopped several feet away. He lifted his goggles and lit his cigar.

"Why, George Groody, isn't it?" O'Reilly sort of gulped, and Groody's mouth widened in that one-sided grin.

He had only met O'Reilly once before and that had been several months ago when he had been in Texas with a circus. He remembered that bull-like bellow which was such a surprise coming from so small a man. It was like the note of a fog horn coming from a tin whistle to hear Penoch O'Reilly talk. O'Reilly came forward, his goggles swinging in his hand.

"You seem to be somewhat knocked off your feet,"

Groody told him, lounging against the side of the ship, cigar in hand.

"I am," came O'Reilly's deep bass voice.

He shook hands absently. He was one of the most unusual looking human beings that Groody or anyone else ever saw, George was thinking. He was just a trifle over five feet tall and possessed the reddest hair and the squarest face extant. Said countenance was garnished with a little mustache, the points of which were always waxed and quirked upward with an effect of cocky self-confidence that was borne out in every move and action of the little flyer. He was like a miniature prize-fighter, with a barrel-like body and trunk-like legs that filled his clothes as though he was poured into them. He gave the impression of being physically hard as a rock, and that impression was absolutely accurate. His wide, blue eyes were large and keen and competent and in his square jawed, pug-nosed face there was plenty to back up the tales which Groody had heard concerning the little adventurer.

"This is Tom Service, Lieutenant Perceval Enoch O'Reilly," Groody introduced them.

"So that's it!" breathed O'Reilly, and when O'Reilly spoke in low tones it was like a shout from someone else.

A MECHANIC HOPPED out of the DeHaviland as two others put wheel blocks under the tires of Groody's ship. The Liberty was idling along smoothly and the mechanic who had walked out with O'Reilly got into the rear seat.

"All right, sir," said the sergeant, saluting. "Do you want your ship gassed and oiled, Lieutenant Groody?"

Groody nodded. Somehow that "Lieutenant" smote

his ears pleasantly. Then his long, narrow, gray eyes shifted again to O'Reilly's distraught face.

"What do you mean—'So that's it?'" he demanded, "You act as though we were a couple of ghosts, or something."

"Hell, no!" boomed O'Reilly, slapping his thigh with his helmet nervously. "It's got nothing to do with you, but I see what they're up to now."

"Yeah? Well, I wish you'd tell us what they're up to," Groody told him.

The chunky Service simply stood by and listened and watched, as was his habit until the going got tough. Then he made up for lost time.

"And if what I think is the truth, damn it, I'm going to squawk until I break their eardrums in Washington!" the rock-like little flyer said grimly.

"You wouldn't have to do more than whisper gently to knock 'em stiff up there," Groody remarked. "What are you sore about, Half Pint?"

"Oh, nothing, and I may be wrong. I knew you were coming to McMullen, but I thought it was on a visit. Then when Graves got there I smelled a rat, and now that Service is along with you, I smell a skunk. No reflection on you, Mr. Service. Ho! Ho! Ho!" That laugh seemed to reverberate around the airdrome.

Tom Service grinned and his round, pink and white face became even more cherubic than before. That's all right," he said gently.

"Well, see you in McMullen. I'm overdue half an hour on patrol as it is," boomed O'Reilly.

He was standing with his short, thick legs spread wide apart as though bracing himself against any blows that the world might offer him. "But you listen to me, George Groody. If what I think's the truth, you're going to run into a riot at McMullen that will make the war seem like a couple of deaf-mutes passing the time of day. Ho! Ho! Ho!"

HE WAVED ONE hand briskly and hopped into his ship. He looked like a flea on a Ferris wheel in the two ton bomber. Despite extra cushions, his head barely cleared the cowling.

"Looks like a midget at the throttle of a locomotive," Groody remarked to Service as he returned the wave of Captain Bush, the Laredo C.O., from the mess hall porch. "Did I ever tell you about that little sucker?"

"A little," nodded Service, as they started toward the mess hall. "He's the fellow that was in the Kosciusko Squadron and then in the Mexican Air Service, and a lot of other places, isn't he?"

"Cocky, hardboiled little egg, at that, and a great guy, according to Slim Evans," Groody nodded. "What do you suppose is biting him?"

"Looks to me," Service said in that cross between a lisp and a stutter, "as t-though he had ambitions to d-do something that he's afraid we've b-been called to do."

Groody, walking along beside his short companion with his customary lounging, bent-kneed stride, gazed down at Tom with a twinkle in his sloping eyes.

"As usual, the well known sleuth has probably socked the nail right on the bean," he stated. "Of course that's it. Hello, Captain! Hi, Jerry! How about a little chow?"

"As a matter of fact," he was thinking as he shook hands with four or five flyers he had known and was introduced to some of the younger pilots whom he didn't know, but who knew of him, "I'm glad this trip's about over myself.

I'm getting a little bit interested in what this junket is all about, and if Graves is already at McMullen, it won't be long now!"

2

AN HOUR AND a half later Groody's monoplane was cleaving its way upward at a climbing angle which made the flyers on the ground start feeling sorry for themselves because they had to fly DeHavilands. Groody drove upward until he had reached five thousand feet and then leveled off for the hour and a half trip to his old station.

There was a curious thrill in every mile that rolled away behind him—it was like coming home once more. Slim Evans and Tex McDowell and Sleepy Spears and Captain Kennard, and all the rest of the old timers with whom he'd eaten and slept and fought and flown were not far away. Sheriff Trowbridge and Major Bill Edwards, and Suite 17 in the McMullen Hotel—he was bound for the only imitation of a home that he had ever had in the last twenty of his thirty odd years.

It was funny how for the last few hours the perennial spiritual hunger for something which he could not quite identify himself had seemed to be temporarily satisfied. All his life, it seemed, he had been seeking and searching for something which was always around the corner, but which eluded him when he came in sight of it. A restless, sometimes savage, discontent had poisoned life for him for many years, and any semi-satisfaction was merely temporary. Now it was as though getting back to McMullen again, plus the stimulating knowledge that events of importance must be close ahead, had dulled that psychological craving within him. He did not remember that it would probably be temporary and that far fields were always greenest to him.

IMMERSED IN ONE of his rare moments of introspection, he was temporarily unconscious of the terrain over which he was flying. Suddenly he felt a grip on his arm and turned to confront Tom Service's gaze. His stocky friend's round blue eyes were curiously brilliant and as Groody's gaze followed Service's pointing finger, it seemed that every muscle stiffened and his heart was curiously constricted.

Three or four miles ahead of them, on the far bank of the river, flames were still licking at the remains of what had been an airplane.

In an instant Groody had nosed the monoplane over and started his dive. There was nothing he could do now, of course, but nevertheless he left the throttle where it was and at close to two hundred miles an hour flashed downward as though haste was a necessity.

"Penoch O'Reilly! The poor little son-of-a-gun!" he was thinking, remembering that the squat aviator was the only one likely to be in that vicinity. Behind his goggles there was a look in his eyes which was not often there. It was a sort of bewildered, wondering pain, and it was the expression of a feeling which often comes to men whose duties are such as to make death not exactly a commonplace but a frequent occurrence. Month after month and year after year friends "went West," and it was as though the rangy flyer wondered why it had to be.

He was flashing up the Rio Grande, barely four hundred

feet high now and any remnant of hope that by some miracle the passengers of the DeHaviland had been saved left him as his ship darted over the wreck. There were the remains of two bodies in it.

"Good God, they were wearing chutes! What happened?" he was thinking.

There was a field which was rough but large enough to permit of a landing, the south end of which was within twenty-five feet of that gruesome bonfire. Perhaps the motor had gone dead and they had tried to make the field, under shot it, and wrecked in the bushes.

"No!" Groody told himself fiercely as he circled around for a landing. If so, it was poor flying, for it so happened that at that point there were three clearings along the Rio Grande of which the one he was about to use was the center one. He could conceive of no position from which the DeHaviland could not have easily reached one of the side clearings.

His ship bumped along the ground. The clearing was sandy and covered with a light growth of sage. Once the nose dipped down and the tail came up as the wheels trundled over a hummock, but they came to rest safely.

The two men unbuckled their belts and unstrapped their parachutes without a word and leaving the motor idling they walked silently toward the wreck.

"Motor half buried," Groody said finally, "and the gas tank exploded! Tom, they just either spun or dived into the ground at about a million miles an hour!"

Service nodded.

"Why didn't they use their chutes?" he asked, his voice low as though out of respect for the charred and blackened corpses which were partially visible beneath a tangle of wire and blackened ash.

THE WRECK WAS still too hot for them to get very close to it, but as though to mark the grave, the rudder had been flung several feet and landed leaning against a bush. It was the rudder of Penoch O'Reilly's DeHaviland and any last hope for the patrolman was snuffed out.

"I guess there's nothing we can do except fan it on to McMullen and give them the news," Groody said quietly. "Listen, Tom, see that motor? It's three feet in the ground! See the position of those bodies right plastered up against it, and the way the tail must have been right in the air, and the whole ship sort of piled up on the motor?"

Service nodded. As he spoke there was no hesitancy in his voice and his words were clear and incisive. This was a phenomenon which always happened when Mr. Tom Service's mind was working on all cylinders.

"It seems to prove that that ship hit in a nose dive or a spin—"

"Nose dive, probably. A spin sometimes isn't so fast unless the motor's left on beside," Groody cut in.

"A straight nose dive, then," Service went on, "from a considerable height or at terrific speed."

"He would have been flying high," Groody said, "and the only thing that could send him into the ground in a nose dive from a considerable altitude would be something like the controls going bad on him. In that case, why didn't they jump in their chutes? If a ship is so badly out of control that it's going to hit the ground the way this baby did, anybody with a grain of sense would jump, and O'Reilly was supposed to be a swell flyer. God knows he's proved it in the last ten years over half the world."

The wreck was still smoldering and the two men started for their idling ship as the first buzzard appeared high in the sky. Groody inserted a cigar in his mouth, his eyes on the ground.

"I'm afraid the old home week won't be such a happy occasion," he said slowly. "Somehow or other, Tom, though, I'd give a lot to know just what the reason for that is back there. Smugglers might have shot O'Reilly in the air, I suppose—"

"The autopsy'll show that," Service reminded him. "I'm wondering a little bit about it myself."

3

IT SEEMED LIKE a long time later that Groody and Service were under the shower baths in the bath houses at the end of the board walk which split the two rows of small square tents representing the living quarters of the McMullen flight. Three ships, one of them carrying Major Searles, the flight surgeon, were on their way to the scene of disaster and a pall of tragedy seemed to rest over the airdrome.

Graves was in town, it appeared. Two of the flyers were on patrol westward, and two more of the dozen flyers and observers who made up the flight were out on patrol east, covering the territory which had marked the end of the trail for O'Reilly.

"I didn't realize that they thought so much of him," Groody was saying as he rubbed down his wiry body with a huge bath towel. The long, flat muscles writhed easily below his skin and it seemed as though he was made of rawhide.

Service, stripped, proved conclusively that in his clothes he was a very deceiving young man. That seemingly corpulent figure was hard and muscular and his wide, sloping shoulders indicated vast reserves of power. He looked what Groody knew him to be, as efficient a rough and tumble fighter as ever survived the none too meticulous mêlées of sailors' dives along the water front or the soirees indulged in by oil field roughnecks in fighting mood.

"It seems like a deserted village," Groody said as they walked up the board walk to their tent in borrowed bathrobes. "There aren't so many of the old gang left, at that. Somehow I've sort of lost interest in what Graves wants with us, although I didn't know O'Reilly very well."

"I imagine," Service said with that gentle vagueness in his eyes and voice, "t-that it's more the mystery about what happened that annoys you than a-anything else, plus the w-way the fellows feel about it, of course."

"Maybe so," Groody said absently. "You said you never met Graves, huh?"

SERVICE SHOOK HIS head as they entered the tent which had been assigned to them. It was chastely furnished with two cots, two tables, two chairs and two sets of clothes hooks.

"B-but I've heard plenty about h-him," he said.

"Well, so have I," Groody told him. "He came rolling into Langham Field from Washington several years ago and used a couple of flyers on a special government mission over in West Virginia, and three times since he's used Border Patrol men, and sometimes the whole patrol, almost taking command of it, to knock off smuggling rings and such like. This may be different, though, because he indicated that he couldn't use an army officer in what's up now. The fact that he's down here, though, seems to mean that the Patrol will be in on it someway."

"Mr. Groody," came a voice from outside.

"Yeah, what is it?"

"Captain Kennard says that Mr. Graves has got in and

he'd like you to come over to headquarters as soon as you get dressed."

"O.K., we'll be there."

It took Service, who was somewhat of a natty dresser, a little longer than Groody to dress. He emerged arrayed as the lilies of the field in double breasted blue serge and a wing collar with a bow tie. Groody had arrayed his lanky body in a pair of flannel trousers and a white shirt which he did not deign to decorate with a necktie, but left comfortably open at the neck.

Somehow he felt a disappointment which he knew it was unworthy of him to feel. He was known far and wide as a hard-boiled and sardonic devil, but somehow he had looked forward with boyish eagerness to dropping in on the old gang again. There were only half a dozen of them left and the news that he and Service had brought had effectually dampened the enthusiasm of their greeting. Suddenly he felt a vast desire to get going on whatever it was they had been asked to come to McMullen for.

He temporarily forgot the events of the morning as they walked toward headquarters, for he had a huge interest in Graves. That he was a power in the Federal service, just how great a power no one seemed to know, Groody had heard, and that he busied himself only with matters of great importance, so far as the Border Patrol knew, was an equal certainty. That he had generated an amount of respect which was rarely paid by the devil-may-care pilots to anyone, and that they seemed somewhat in awe of him, meant the last touch to the legend which had been built up around him.

As Groody told Service, "I get the idea, in talking to

some of the boys that knew him well when he was down here before, that they'd think a hell of a lot of him if he ever let them get close enough to him to indicate it. He seems to be a cross between Machiavelli and one of the Twelve Apostles, as far as they're concerned."

"W-well, we'll soon see."

THEY WENT INTO headquarters, one of the short row of white painted buildings which bounded the southern edge of the airdrome, and Captain Kennard greeted them from the outside office. He was dictating a wire to the sergeant-major. The stocky, bow-legged, scarred-faced little C.O. was not exactly himself. Three men of the flight had been killed in the last two months, and the doughty captain was upset.

"I'll be with you in a second," he said in his raucous voice. "Mr. Graves is inside."

Groody waited restlessly as the captain finished his telegrams to general headquarters and the home address of O'Reilly.

"Well," the captain said with a forced smile as he got up, "sure is hell for you to get back to the old stamping ground under circumstances like this, George."

He ran his hand through the mouse colored pompadour which was like so many spikes on his head. His square face, bearing the marks of more airplane wrecks than any known flyer had ever survived in the memory of the Air Service, took on a look of determined cheerfulness.

"I wish we could postpone this little conversation until the boys get back and I could get it off my mind, but might as well try to stop the Twentieth Century with a pasteboard fence as this Graves guy when he's got something to do. Come on in."

He led the way into the inside office with Groody following him. A man of medium height with iron gray hair arose from a chair.

"Mr. Graves, may I present Mr. Groody and Mr. Service," barked Captain Kennard. "I guess you all know enough about each other to allow me to sit down and shut up from now on."

"How do you do, sir?" said Groody as he shook hands.

Graves merely smiled. Somehow it seemed that when his long-fingered hand grasped Groody's sinewy one, a sort of galvanizing current flowed from the immaculately attired government agent. Groody got the impression of a broad browed, almost ascetic face, made remarkable by a pair of the most brilliant gray eyes he had ever seen. They were very large and wide set and seemed to glow with a warm illumination which made him curiously attractive. Down to the cheekbones the face was unusually wide, but below that point it seemed to fall away sharply to a thin, cleft jaw. Thick, smoothly brushed iron gray hair lay close to his head and as he smiled he looked like some scholarly man who might be an eminent doctor or lawyer. His shoulders were unusually broad and his clothes breathed good taste and a good tailor.

GRAVES TURNED TO shake hands with Service and as his profile came into view Groody was conscious of a real shock. He was lighting a cigar, but his sloping eyes never left the countenance before him. It was as though by some species of magic the man had completely changed faces. Seen from the side his forehead receded sharply from the prominent temples and his nose turned into something very much like the beak of a bird of prey. Below it his well cut lips seemed unusually thin, and the chin receded. What seemed from the front to be a wide, thoughtful, kindly countenance turned into a keen, ruthless face which seemed to fairly shriek aggressiveness and a sort of cold ferocity. If ever Groody had seen a man who looked like the born man hunter, it was Graves in profile.

"Sit down, gentlemen," Graves said. "It was good of you to gamble your time on a note so vague as mine, but at the time I could not be definite. Cigarette, Captain? You, Mr. Service?"

His speech was cultivated and precise and his voice held a warmth which seemed akin to that in his eyes. Bushy gray eyebrows, which from the side seemed to overhang like miniature cliffs, were from the front a sort of distinguished frame which lent impressiveness to those remarkable eyes. It was really hard to connect the smiling man who was looking at Groody with the man he had just seen shaking hands with Service.

Tom was sitting to one side and Groody chuckled inwardly as he noticed that even that blasé young man was scrutinizing Graves with a mixture of bewilderment and interest. He took off his glasses and polished them absently, which was a sure sign that he was trying to think something through.

"In the first place," Graves said, "are you gentlemen free for say a month to accept a proposition which involves a fairly generous amount of money for your services, plus I may add, in fairness, a certain amount of danger?"

"Well, sir, that depends on what it is," Groody found

himself saying, and could not tell for the life of him why that "sir" had come from him unconsciously. Somehow Graves automatically rated it.

"It would be somewhat along the lines of what you have been dabbling in since Mr. Service left his government work and embarked on his individual career," Graves said smilingly. "I am very familiar with your work with the Levin-Willet carnival and the circus, and in various other places since Mr. Service inlisted your aid, and I may say that his record as an army intelligence man during the war and with the government afterward is the principal reason why the proposition is made to you. Plus, I may say, your own ability along that line, Mr. Groody, but more important in your case is the fact that you are a flyer. You are free, if it appeals to you?"

"Yes, sir," said Service, and now his round blue eyes were very bright as they rested unwinkingly on the contained Graves.

"WELL, THEN," GRAVES said and it seemed as though his body, without movement, gave the impression of leaning forward tensely, "I hope that it appeals to you. Not only the fact that you have worked together, combining your talents, but the fact that you are lifelong friends will make you uniquely valuable to the government. There is an outlaw in Mexico, the leader of a band of aerial smugglers, named Count Friederich Von Sternberg—"

"Oh-ho!" breathed Groody.

"Captain Kennard and other men like Lieutenant Evans, can tell you more about him than I can, and Lieutenant O'Reilly, had he not been so tragically killed, could have given even more details, but I can sketch him in now enough for our purpose," Graves went on, and suddenly Groody was aware of a certain irresistible drive in the man.

"Count Von Sternberg was one of the leading German aces during the war. Perhaps you, Lieutenant Groody, heard of him while you were in France."

Groody nodded, but Graves scarcely noticed it. He was talking ahead as though nothing could stop his smooth and orderly progress toward the goal which he was seeking.

"He was a remarkable man in the German air service and has proved to be even more extraordinary in many respects during the years since the war. A part of his menace, as well as the explanation for his being the thorn in the side of the United States which he is, is due to his peculiar make up. I believe I can say with absolute certainty that there has never arisen in the annals of Mexico and the United States an individual of such menace to the friendly relations between the two countries as he, although the general public may not know it, and I say that taking into full consideration the history of Mexican bandits, from Villa up and down."

4

GROODY WAS LOUNGING in his chair, every muscle relaxed, and a cigar drooping from his fingers. His face, however, was alive with interest and his usually drooping eyelids had lowered until his eyes were mere slits of light in his head. With every word that Graves said his interest was mounting. An ordinary outlaw was one thing, but Graves' words seemed to hint at matters far more important than a few smuggled immigrants or dope.

"You'll learn more about him if and when you go to work," Graves went on in his modulated voice. "However, I can tell you this. He was apparently a fanatic in the World War, believing wholeheartedly that the Fatherland was one hundred per cent right in everything. And, following the war, he found himself financially ruined. A year of drifting around the world as an adventurer brought him to Mexico, which has a large German population, and he joined the Mexican Air Service as an instructor.

"He is a man of force, personality and some charm. The principal thing which has molded his conduct since then, according to our investigations around Mexico City and various other parts of Mexico, is that he blames the United States for the defeat of Germany and the idea seems to have grown in his mind that he'll conduct a one man war, as it were, against us. His endeavor has been, apparently, to embarrass this government in every way possible. What better way could there be than to keep Mexico and the United States in a constant state of friction?

A GREAT MANY of his endeavors along the Border have seemed to be undertaken with the idea of financial profit secondary. His main purpose has been, it seems obvious to me, to get us into trouble with Mexico."

"Slim Evans described him best, I think," Captain Kennard put in. "He says that Von Sternberg has an ambition to be a wild hair in Uncle Sam's beard."

Graves nodded unsmilingly as Groody grinned.

"That's about what Slim would say," commented Groody.

"Failing in getting us into trouble with Mexico," Graves went on, not noticing the interruption, "he has attempted several things which would make this country ridiculous. He gives the effect of wanting to thumb his nose at the United States whenever possible and show us how ignorant and thickheaded we are.

"Take the case of probably his most famous attempted coup. He almost succeeded in stealing the dirigible *America*, when it was moored to the mooring mast in El Paso."

Groody grinned and again that eager, boyish quality showed through, as life seemed to be opening up rapidly ahead, revealing vistas of pleasure and profit.

"I remember that," he stated. "Had his men disguised as photographers and newspaper men, didn't he? Took off with the pride of the navy and was only stopped because Slim and this little Penoch O'Reilly were still aboard the balloon."

"Exactly," Graves nodded. "He was captured, badly injured, but he finally escaped with the help of confederates from the hospital at Fort Bliss. However, putting aside the various times when his aerial smuggling across the Border has been forestalled—of course, no one knows exactly how many times he has succeeded—he has, within the last year, grown into a unique and almost unprecedented figure in Mexico and he bids fair to attain his ambition. That ambition, as I have said, is to keep the United States and Mexico in a constant state of uproar. He has been responsible, probably, for as many diplomatic notes in the last year as Pancho Villa in his prime. When and if you go to Mexico, you'll get more details than I can give you."

"Oh, I see the lay," Groody said.

HE GLANCED OVER at Tom. That chunky young man had removed his glasses once again and was polishing them with a beatific expression on his square countenance.

"I'll say this, however," Graves said, and a hint of a smile was tugging at his lips as he saw the reaction of the two men, "he has developed down there what amounts to a small army, that army including an unknown number of airplanes, manned by flying soldiers of fortune of all nations. The oil boom several years ago in the Tampico fields was tremendous, of course, and right after the war Mexico drew to it a great number of adventurers. The Germans are popular in Mexico, anyway, as versus Americans, and Von Sternberg seems to be of the type and personality which appeals to the Mexicans, particularly the peons. He has made himself, one might say, a flying Pancho Villa. He has various lairs back in the most remote fastnesses of Mexico, from all we can gather, and no one knows how many hundreds, perhaps thousands, of peons are loosely connected with his organization. He has made himself a Robin Hood, as it were, and there are many thousand people in Mexico who are not actively connected with him but who chuckle over and sympathize with his exploits.

"Last, and most significant, his illegal activities are confined, apparently, to two things. One of them is harrying the Border here. The second is harrying the American and English oil companies which are operating in the vast Tampico fields. He touches neither Mexicans nor Germans."

"What does he do?" Service asked suddenly, peering owlishly at Graves through his glasses.

"Robs their payrolls, principally," Graves told him tersely. "There have been two outlaws down in that country since the days of Villa who have operated somewhat along the same lines. One of them, Marty Morrison, a red-headed Texan, was not a flyer, and after being squeezed by one of the big oil companies, annoyed them tremendously for years with a group of ground bandits. He, like Von Sternberg, had two things in his favor. His personality appealed to the Mexicans, and more than that, the fact that he harried the more or less hated American capitalists appealed secretly to a large number of our southern friends who resent the development of the fields by foreigners. He operated for years, until he did a few things like blowing up a railroad train, and was finally hunted down. He was shot and his body laid in state in the public square of Tampico for a week. Thousands and thousands of peons made pilgrimages to see it. That may give you a slight idea of the status of the right kind of a bandit who annoys Americans in that country."

GROODY THREW BACK his head and laughed, and he rarely laughed aloud. His brown hair, parted on the side, became wildly ruffled as he ran his fingers through it delightedly.

"That's where a man gets credit for what he does," he said sardonically.

"The next one was a young fellow named Delroy who worked alone and whose purpose was to get back the money big business had legally stolen from himself and his brother on some oil property. He led everyone a merry chase but finally returned the money and has settled down to respectability once more.

"However, neither of these men were comparable to Von Sternberg in possibility of harm. Conditions in the oil field country are such that Americans are tolerated, not welcomed, and it would be difficult to say what proportion of the common people of Mexico within a radius of hundreds of miles of Tampico secretly sympathize with Von Sternberg. He has become a legend, and one of the proudest things a peon can tell his children is that he has laid eyes on 'The Cloud Rider,' which is what the Mexicans call him. Von Sternberg scrupulously pays them for anything he may get, such as a steer to kill, or anything of that sort, and he robs, as I said before, only Americans.

"During the reign of Marty Morrison the companies started flying their payrolls around the field by airplane to avoid being held up by Morrison and his men. Now even that does no good. Von Sternberg's secret service system would be a credit to a small nation, apparently, and his inside information seems to have no limits.

"It has resulted in the oil companies down there being

in a very wrought up condition. It has been a matter for diplomatic correspondence and the Mexican Government seems to be helpless. However, they are officially cooperating with us and we have permission to take active, though secret, steps to protect our interests down there. We want things secret to avoid working up the common people of that district. If they had knowledge of the fact that United States officers were officially invading Mexico, as it were, there would be much friction."

"Just exactly what do you want us to do?" Service inquired crisply.

"Go down there, have Mr. Groody take a job as a flyer carrying the payrolls, you have another excuse, work with one of my men who is also a flyer, Robert Daly, and with every cooperation from us, every cooperation, that is, which does not involve showing our hand too much, hunt Von Sternberg down, dead or alive."

FOR A MOMENT there was silence in the small, bare office. Captain Kennard was tilted back in his chair, his booted feet on the desk and his eyes on the ceiling. A far away drone reached Groody's ears, but with his mind busy with the vista which had been opened up to him, he did not note its significance. Suddenly a thought occurred to him.

"Listen, Tom," he exploded, "maybe that's what O'Reilly meant down at Laredo when we saw him. Wasn't he in the Mexican Air Service, Captain? Did he and Von Sternberg—"

"Yes," nodded the captain, "they knew each other and were deadly enemies. I—"

"Listen!"

That drone had now become a sort of angry buzz.

"There come the boys back now with the bodies," Kennard said. "I guess I'll have to adjourn myself from this meeting for a little while, Mr. Graves."

"We all will," Graves said crisply. "It will give Mr. Service and Mr. Groody an opportunity to think things over."

The homing airplanes were now very close to the field and the roar of the three Liberties was becoming almost deafening. Groody peered out the window.

"They're diving in," he said slowly, and, as the group remembered the tragic cargo they were carrying, there was no urge to conversation. They went out silently. At the door of the outer office, as the first ship was gliding in, Groody said absently, as though to get his mind off the situation, "How does that sound to you, Tom?"

"O.K. with me," nodded one of the best investigators the United States had ever had.

They walked out to the line without further conversation. Graves remained on the porch as though unwilling to intrude himself in the grief of the flight.

The enlisted men of the squadron were lined up in orderly rank close to the two hearses from town which were grim reminders of what those ships were carrying in. Graves noticed with surprise that a row of automobiles holding curious, quiet civilians from McMullen were drawn up before the hangars. One girl was crying and a woman who was evidently her mother was trying to comfort her.

"O'Reilly had friends, of course," Graves thought. "So had the other poor devil, I suppose."

Back in the old days the town's people had adopted the flight which had come to be their pride and joy, and there was nothing surprising in the fact that two or three hundred McMullenites had turned out.

THE SHIPS, FLOWN by Slim Evans, Tex McDowell and Sleepy Spears, taxied up to the line and in dead silence two ghastly bags were lifted tenderly from the rear cockpit and put into the hearses. They drove off slowly toward town and, as though actuated by the same impulse, the civilian cars got under way. They filed out behind the hearses as though to pay a last tribute of respect to the dead men.

"I wonder what all the chatter is about," the somber Groody thought to himself.

That knot of officers clustered around the towering form of Slim Evans seemed to be talking with more gesticulations than the occasion warranted. Suddenly, for what reason he knew not, Groody found his heart pounding faster. They were coming toward him now, Slim Evans, who was nearly six feet six inches tall and as thin as a fishing rod, in the center. Beside him pattered dried-up, bespectacled little Major Searls, the kindly flight surgeon. Kennard was apparently firing question after question at them. Tex McDowell lounged along, keeping pace easily, and Sleepy Spears, his shorter legs working fast and with unwonted energy, was talking with what seemed like real enthusiasm. Tom Service was listening, as always.

Groody, who had seen them all briefly when he had landed, got up and walked over to meet them like a ruminative crane. His dark face held no tinge of the customary mockery in it. Graves, up on the porch, was watching that chattering group curiously, too, and the enlisted men had broken ranks and were talking excitedly.

"Why all the chatter?" Groody inquired from a distance of fifteen feet.

Slim Evans' thin face was a setting for a pair of sun-crinkled eyes which were now blazing with interest. The group were at the foot of headquarters steps vow and Graves was leaning over the railing.

"Plenty to chatter about," Slim stated, gesturing spaciously. "That was Penoch O'Reilly's ship, all right, and there were two men in it, but neither one of them was Penoch O'Reilly!"

5

FOR A SECOND Groody's lanky body seemed turned into stone. His cigar was lifted halfway to his lips and there it stayed. Suddenly his face seemed harsher and that sweeping line around one corner of his mouth deepened. Then he asked, "How come?"

"Let's get into the office and talk things over," Kennard snapped. "This may have something to do with your job, Groody. Mr. Graves, will you come in with us?"

As they trooped into the office Groody fell in alongside of Service. There was not in all the world a man, who, in the more extraordinary vicissitudes of life, Groody would rather have at his right hand than Service. Vapid looking, seeming to be fat and flabby and vacuous, he was more than the son of a former distinguished statesman. He was one of the best minds, if not the best, along certain lines, that Groody had ever come in contact with. He spoke five languages and could fight in any language. He had a mind like a steel trap, and when he was at work on a problem there was an effect of inevitability about him as he ruthlessly followed the facts to a conclusion which often had escaped everyone else.

THE TWO HAD been together for three years up to the time the war had separated them, and, from the forecastle of a South Sea tramp to jail in Shanghai, Groody had seen Tom

Service operate. The fundamental bond which held them together was a restless discontent and a deep-seated love for strange places and extraordinary emergencies. There was in that stocky, immaculately dressed, bespectacled chap alongside him the heart of a Columbus.

"What do you think, Tom?" Groody whispered as they went into the office.

"I d-don't know what to think, y-yet," Service told him with a suspicion of a lisp. Nevertheless he was polishing his glasses as they ranged themselves around the walls.

"Now, let's get this straight," Kennard said, his jaw outthrust. "Major, you're sure of what you're saying?"

"Absolutely, Captain," the little major answered earnestly. "Just for one item of proof I collected a complete set of bones of the upper arms of both men, and the legs. O'Reilly was such a small man that there can be no doubt that both of the men killed in that plane were at least eight inches taller than Penoch."

"And there's no doubt that it was O'Reilly's ship?"

"No," drawled Tex McDowell, lounging against the wall. "By some miracle the number on the motor even wasn't blotted out and the rudder never got scratched. We brought it along."

Graves was over in a corner, his eyes like two searchlights, but he said nothing.

Kennard wheeled on Groody.

"You say Penoch and Gravesend took off," he barked, "half an hour before you did?"

Groody nodded.

"When you saw the wreck, how long before you saw it do you think it happened?"

"The flames had just about died out," Groody told him. "I don't know—how long does a ship burn after the tank explodes, ordinarily—twenty minutes or a half an hour?"

"That all depends," Kennard said tersely. "Any sign of another ship?"

"We looked around," Slim Evans told him, "and couldn't even see anything which would prove it. There were some marks that might have been wheels and skid marks, but the sand was soft and there was a little breeze, and so it's hard to tell. And another thing, there wasn't a sign of a parachute in the ship."

"They both had 'em on when they left Laredo," Groody interrupted.

"There were no bullet marks in the bodies, Major?" Graves said suddenly.

"No, sir," Searles declared.

"Furthermore," Tex McDowell said, "we scoured the country after we got the bodies aboard for at least fifteen miles in every direction. There wasn't a sign of Penoch or a parachute. We went over Mexico, too. I suppose that's another smack on the beezer of International Law.

"What about this Gravesend, the mechanic?" Tom Service asked quietly. "Anybody know him well?"

"Been here a year, was a sergeant, good army record and all O.K. as far as I know," Kennard shot back at him.

"Did Gravesend ask to go on the patrol?" Service asked.

FOR A MOMENT there was silence. Then Pop Cravath, the roly-poly, bald-headed adjutant spoke up.

"No. Due to shortage of men we've been using a couple of the older sergeants as reserves. It was Gravesend's regular turn and I ordered him to go."

"What are you getting at, Service?" demanded Kennard.

A portion of Service's record was known to them all and consequently his opinion demanded respect.

"I was trying to connect up the fact that O'Reilly was in the Mexican Air Service with Von Sternberg and what you said a few minutes ago about their being enemies," Service said incisively. "There are dozens of things that could have happened, but any of them need a strong motive behind them, and there are arguments against each one of them."

"Now that the matter of Von Sternberg has been brought up," Graves said smoothly, "suppose we go over to the recreation hall where everyone can sit down, and discuss the matter."

As they walked over to the recreation hall, which was in the next building, it seemed that every one of the khaki clad flyers, and Graves, Groody and Service as well, were too busy with their own speculations to do any talking. They disposed themselves about the comfortable room, which held several easy chairs, a magazine covered table, a phonograph and a piano. Graves, as though by natural right, leaned against the table at the head of the room alongside of Captain Kennard.

"As Mr. Service said," he stated quietly, "many things could have happened, but all of them that I can think of are unlikely at the moment, and are unexplainable. I should like to know, Captain Kennard, the exact status of Lieutenant O'Reilly and Count Von Sternberg."

"Slim knows more about that than anybody else. He and O'Reilly were pals," Kennard said crisply.

Groody's eyes narrowed with surprise. That was one of the unusual things about Groody's appearance. When most people's jaw would have dropped and their eyes widened with astonishment, his mouth became tighter, that droop on one corner became lower and the drooping lids almost hid his eyes.

"There's more to this than meets the eye," he was thinking. "I didn't know there was a personal tie-up between the genial Heine and McMullen."

Now that he came to think of it, however, there had been various times when the public prints had hinted about a brush between aerial smugglers and the McMullen flight.

"You all know about as much as I do except for one thing," Evans said, his Adam's apple popping up and down his long neck like a monkey on a string. "Penoch was in the Mexican Air Service with Von Sternberg before he got back into the American Army. You all know what a fire brand Penoch was, as hard-boiled a little egg as ever lived, and he fought his way through the world in every sort of a spot from canvasman with a circus to the Kosciusko Squadron.

AS I GOT it from Penoch, Von Sternberg was cock of the walk down there and Penoch ran afoul of him over a girl. I think Von Sternberg acted like a rat toward a girl Penoch thought a lot of. Then Von Sternberg got him into trouble, bad trouble, got him taken captive by a half bandit, half general down there, through his influence, and in the end Penoch had to kill that Mexican half bandit, half general named Ferrara to make his getaway. Then the whole thing just about ruined Penoch in addition to putting him through quite an extended period of plain, ordinary hell when he figured his life wasn't worth a nickel.

"Anyway, Penoch's situation when he came here,

although none of us knew it at the time, was that he was more or less in danger of his life if anybody knew he was here. This Ferrara had a bunch of fanatic followers, and four or five of them would have trailed Penoch to China, if they'd known where he was, to avenge their chief.

"Then a couple of little matters came along that you all remember and I don't need to go into, Mr. Graves, in which Penoch was mainly responsible for spoiling Von Sternberg's plans to give Uncle Sam's beard a tweak or two. Von Sternberg got wise to the fact that he was here and meanwhile just got to hate him more, I guess, because he'd continued to interfere with the Count's plans.

"Well, he had Penoch right by the left ear. If he tipped off Ferrara's men, and I think Von Sternberg, after he got to be an outlaw, took over most of Ferrara's old gang, Penoch's life on the Border wouldn't be worth a nickel, and Penoch loved this patrol and being an officer in it better than anything else he'd ever done. So the little squirt was running around here worried stiff, worried to an extent that none of you know, but I'm going to tell you now. You remember, of course, the time that Von Sternberg showed up here in person? That is, you don't remember it, but I told you about it. You know about it, too, Mr. Graves, but it may be news to Tom and George."

"What?" snapped Service. "He showed up here at McMullen?"

Slim nodded.

"I'll say he did. Penoch hadn't been himself for weeks. Acted like a man possessed. I happened to be officer of the day when the whole gang, except me and Penoch, were away. I came walking down the tents, heard voices in Penoch's tent, shoved my head in, and there sat Von Sternberg."

"Well, I'll be damned!" breathed Groody.

HE WAS LEANING forward like an eagle prepared to take off, and for the first time since the proposition to take Von Sternberg's trail had been mentioned, he was utterly and entirely enthralled. Something in the thought of that visit into the lair of the enemy suddenly made the German become alive to him.

"Well, I was knocked deader than a herring for a minute," Slim went on, "but that's neither here nor there. It came out right then that Von Sternberg held Penoch's life in his hand if he wanted to shoot off his mouth, and he'd been blackmailing Penoch, not for the small amount of money that Penoch could raise for him, but to break him. Von Sternberg said plainly that his revenge for the things Penoch had been instrumental in doing to him would be simply this: to drag Penoch down financially and every other way until he was a wreck and in disgrace and then—get this—his object was to force Penoch to join his, the Count's, bunch of bandits and become an outlaw. Sweet little methodical revenge, eh? Not that Penoch wouldn't have been a damn good man, if he wanted to be crooked, for Von Sternberg's purposes."

For a minute there was silence as Groody and Service digested this morsel of information. It came, evidently, as no surprise to the others, Groody noticed.

"Now git this, Tom, and you, too, George," Slim went on after lighting a cigarette, "I know damn well why you're here, you lucky devils. Von Sternberg had a man with him when he visited Penoch, and after this interview was over—I don't need to say that Penoch and I were under guns—Von Sternberg forced us to help him steal a ship. He made the unusual proposition of not tying us up or anything on our word not to do anything to stop him until he was off the ground. We had a faster ship here then than the DeHaviland he took, so Penoch and I chased him down into Mexico, and what do you think the cagey devil had in mind? To lure us over there, that was it! There were three ships waiting for us. We got into a hell of a fight and finally both Penoch and I escaped, but his object was as plain as the nose on my face, and that's plain enough. He was going to kidnap O'Reilly, that's what he was going to do. Get him down there in that bunch, and then God knows what—not kill him or anything, but just force Penoch into enough so that he'd have burned his bridges behind him and couldn't do anything but stay.

"And now I'm going to break a confidence. This is news to the whole gang of you."

THE TALL FLYER shifted slightly and every eye turned toward him. Groody was aware of the fact that suddenly life seemed a very glorious thing. He was listening with such absorbed attention that he had forgotten where he was, forgotten all the many personal problems which had dogged his steps for years, and was living only in the moment. He was like a snake ready to spring and his sloping eyes were glinting with a sort of cold light that turned them into streaks of silver across his face.

"I found out that night how far Von Sternberg had gone with Penoch," Evans said slowly, "and you all know Penoch well enough to know that it means the menace of Von Sternberg wasn't exaggerated by the little devil. He was paying tribute to Von Sternberg and figuring and figuring how in the world he could get a chance to kill him. Just marking time, and getting further and further into the swamp.

"To make a long story short, he sold his car to a major up at Donovan, I forget his name, and the major was to pay him the first of the month. On the strength of that, and being desperate, Penoch—he was mess officer, George—stole a thousand dollars from the mess fund to give to Von Sternberg to hold him off a little while longer, and figured to repay it when he got the dough for his car. Then the major got killed. I loaned Penoch the thousand bucks—I had a little oil dough left over then—to fix up the mess fund, and never said a word about it, but there's no doubt about this: first, O'Reilly is and has been scared to death of Von Sternberg, and will be as long as Von Sternberg's alive. That little hellion has seen plenty and done plenty and he may have strayed a long ways further off the beaten track than we give him credit for, out in the jungle somewhere.

"Number two, it's one of Von Sternberg's ambitions to make Penoch O'Reilly into an outlaw, to break him, as it were, and take everything away from him that he wants or values. Does that throw any light on what may have happened in that wreck today?"

"Certainly," Graves said quietly, and Groody felt rather than observed the effortless way in which the prestige and personality of the man before them automatically dominated the others. It seemed that each man stiffened and his eyes focused on Graves as though by magnetic attraction as he went on to outline his conception of what had happened to Penoch O'Reilly.

"It would not be unusual, in view of Von Sternberg's past history, for him to know the approximate time of O'Reilly's patrol, or to get information in other ways. On some pretext O'Reilly was caused to land—perhaps another ship in distress. Upon landing, one or perhaps two of Von Sternberg's men are waiting. O'Reilly is captured, one outlaw flies his ship with the mechanic still in the back seat, and O'Reilly is taken in the outlaw ship. An accident happens or perhaps Gravesend, if he was loyal, made some move which resulted in the wreck, in an attempt to save the ship. The matter of parachutes might be accounted for by the fact that O'Reilly retained his and that the other Von Sternberg man took Gravesend's. That is but one of many possibilities, and that may color your work in Mexico," Graves concluded, his remarkable eyes flitting from Service to Groody.

EVANS MOVED RESTLESSLY in the momentary silence. Then, "I hate like hell to say it," he said, "but it's only fair to you boys to mention this. The wreck I can't explain—"

"No, and it doesn't hold water," Kennard barked suddenly. "Sergeant Gravesend could fly well enough. Of course the controls could have gone bad, or something like that, but they'd have left Gravesend on the ground and not taken a potential traitor to their cause with them unless Gravesend was already one of them. It would have been much more simple to leave him out in the mesquite. He was in the back seat, was he not, Major Searles?"

"Yes, sir."

"No evidence of being tied?" Graves slid in.

"No, sir."

"Well, anyway," Slim blurted, "it's only fair, as I say, for me to say this. O'Reilly was in a bad way. It may be that he didn't need any persuasion to join in some skulduggery out there in the mesquite, and he may have joined up voluntarily. A man can only fight so long. If he did that, though, I firmly believe it was with the purpose of waiting his chance to knock off the Count. On the other hand, that may not be it at all. He may have just decided to chuck everything and throw in with Von Sternberg."

"Either one of which," Service pointed out quietly, "will make our job more difficult. If O'Reilly is a prisoner he could be used in an emergency as a hostage, so to speak, his life the forfeit for any definite move against Von Sternberg. Incidentally, he seemed very much wrought up over the fact that George and I were on our way to McMullen. He knew what the proposition we would be offered was, I think."

"And it made him sore as hell," Groody said.

There was much more conversation as the quick Texas twilight fell without anyone really noticing it enough even to light the lights, and at the end of an hour Groody said his say.

"I guess we're set to leave from Nuevo Laredo on the first train, ain't we, Tom?" he inquired.

Service nodded and his eyes somehow were like a cat's in the semi-gloom.

"In v-view of all the events, y-yes," he said mildly.

"You lucky devils!" Slim Evans and Lieutenant Tex McDowell said simultaneously.

"I'm sorry we can't use you boys, but you would be too well known to the man we're after," Graves reminded them.

It was not half an hour later, though, when that point seemed to be of no importance.

MOST OF THE group had adjourned to the porch of the recreation building, and low stars which seemed to be studding a purple canopy were winking out when a familiar drone reached the ears of the flyers. It was coming from the north, and in a moment the fire from the exhaust pipes of a ship coming in low and fast over the mesquite was visible.

"Must be somebody from Donovan making a late trip," Kennard remarked.

The newly installed landing searchlight bathed the airdrome in a wan light as the on-coming ship dipped down as though to land.

"About time he cut his motor," Sleepy Spears remarked.

With mounting wonder not unmixed with misgivings, Groody watched the strange ship come darting across the airdrome. It was a monoplane. It couldn't be any army ship. Was the pilot taking a look at the field before landing? He was coming straight for the steps and making at feast two hundred miles an hour. The pilot himself could not be seen behind the shielding motor.

Just as the amazed group of airmen were about to scurry for cover the ship tilted up in a bank. The lower wing was almost digging into the ground as it shot upward in as daring a chandelle as Groody had ever looked upon. A split second later the pilot's face leaped into view under the rays of the landing searchlight. His goggles were raised to his helmet as though to permit himself to be identified more readily.

"Good God!" yelled Slim Evans. "It's Penoch O'Reilly!"

In that quick moment Groody got an impression that

O'Reilly was staring unwinkingly at the flyers. He waved his arm as though in derision, and the ship shot away southward over the buildings.

There was no sense in trying to chase him, and he did not return.

6

THE LITTLE WHITE fruit steamer, *Pride of Galveston*, was making its way slowly up the Rio Panuco under the guidance of a Mexican pilot, and Messrs. Groody and Service, supposedly deck hands on the boat, were leaning over the rail watching the panorama of the stately river.

Days had elapsed since the apparition of Penoch O'Reilly in McMullen, and many and divers steps had been taken under the supervision of Graves to assure the fact that the arrival of Groody and Service would be a very unostentatious one.

"We ought to be in sight of Tampico in a moment," Service was saying mildly. "C-Certainly looks as though they were t-taking some oil out of this country, doesn't it?"

Groody nodded. The ship had passed a seemingly unending series of great tank farms and shipping terminals. The slopes on either side of the river were covered with great fifty-five thousand barrel tanks, and at the docks below them, black oil freighters were taking aboard their loads to carry to the four corners of the earth.

THE RIVER ITSELF, as the ship nosed its way toward the as yet unseen city, was a colorful sight. Water craft of every description, mostly of an ancient vintage, scurried across the surface of the river, carrying people of all sorts back and forth across it. There was a stern-wheeler making its slow way with a cargo of chattering peons, several flat barges which barely moved and which were apparently carrying laborers across the river, and fast little motor boats carrying oil men about their business.

"Well, it won't be long now," Groody remarked. "Do you suppose we're going to get away with coming in this way, even if O'Reilly has spilled the beans?"

"T-that remains to be seen," Service said gently.

"I'm curious for a look at this flyer, Robert Daly, that's to work with us down here," Groody said. "He sounds O.K., but in a deal like this I certainly like to know my man."

"As l-long as Graves put him on the job with us," Service said mildly, "I don't b-believe we've got to worry. W-what I'm wondering about is how much he's b-been able to do up to now. I never saw anything l-like the confidence that Graves seems to have in him. We're practically in h-his hands."

Groody nodded.

"Well, we can change that, if necessary," he said. "God, I'd give a couple of days off my life to know exactly where Penoch O'Reilly's at! I wake up at night thinking about it. Where and how did he get that ship? Why was he coming in from the north? Why did he keep on going, and where is he, and why? Thomas, my boy, we may be in a very perilous position. Do you realize that?"

His lips widened in that sardonic grin, and it would have been apparent to an onlooker, had there been any, that the perilous position held certain elements of enjoyment for the lanky adventurer.

Mr. Service nodded.

"L-looks to me as though there was Tampico," he said gently.

"Complete with buzzards, and all that it takes to keep them alive, it looks like," Groody put in. "I have a feeling, Thomas, that if it weren't for this breeze, we'd have smelled the town before we saw it."

For a moment the two were silent as they took in the scene. The interest of it to Groody was heightened subconsciously by the thought in the back of his mind that there, on top of that hill, there undoubtedly lay the secrets they were there to uncover.

Along the river front were hundreds of little shacks, some of them built on stilts in the water, and most of them apparently thrown together with all sorts of salvaged material—rolling planks, pieces of board scarcely a foot square, even tin cans and adobe had been used to make up a ram-shackled little river front section which expressed unutterable filth and squalor.

THE CITY ITSELF was on the hill, and between the river front and the city proper the most prominent feature was what looked like a huge, covered public market. Across the river lay the great terminal of the Texas Company, and close to them, as the ship nosed in, were the huge docks and government buildings. There were at least seven or eight sizeable ocean-going vessels lined up at the docks, which caused Service to remark:

"I seem to vaguely r-remember that this port does m-more business than any other in the world, with two or three exceptions. However, I m-may be wrong."

"Well, let's prepare to make ready to begin to start," Groody suggested. "You're going to the Hacienda Hotel, as I understand it, and register, while I go direct to Daly's room there. I wonder if that's the hotel? It must be." He was pointing to a huge white building standing out in bold relief to the left of the city as they were looking at it. His eyes searched the side of the building and soon picked up the letters. "Yes, that is it. Well, we won't even have to hire a taxi cab now. Did you arrange with the captain to get our junk delivered inconspicuously?"

Service nodded.

"Everything is set. In order t-to make it look right, in case of s-spies, we'd better stay until the unloading is done, I presume."

Which they did. The dock was a colorful conglomeration of peons in all sorts of nondescript clothing, the only standard articles of which were huge straw sombreros and bright colored bandannas. Many of them were barefooted and occasionally a woman, whose feet were in the same state of nudity, passed by selling sweetmeats and nuts.

The main part of the *Pride of Galveston's* cargo was booked for Vera Cruz, so it was only two hours before Groody, still wearing a uniform cap which bore the words *Pride of Galveston,* walked down the gangplank, went through a few brief and at least temporarily deceptive official formalities, and then proceeded to lounge his way up the dusty road which led to the city on top of the hill.

He kept the hotel in sight and made his way toward it through a series of hilly, narrow streets which were lined with booths that sold everything from shoes to liquor. Such novelty as there was in the scene completely wore off, for Groody was very much accustomed to Mexican manners and ways, and he quickened his pace despite the enervating heat, as though he could not wait to meet Daly.

HE WAS THINKING of what he had heard about the man who was to be their ally. That he was a former flyer, and before that had had a checkered career as everything from a professional gambler to a race track betting commissioner, was all in his favor. That Graves, and even the other boys, had so much confidence in him was also. His record as a flyer right on the Border Patrol was one hundred per cent excellent, and yet somehow Groody had sensed a certain reservation in the words of the men who had known Robert Daly, otherwise known as the Duke. It wasn't dislike and it wasn't distrust. It was rather bewilderment, and it had aroused Groody's curiosity.

He walked into the big lobby and was relieved to find three or four people sitting about. He lounged over and bought some Mexican cigarettes unconcernedly and inquired for the location of Room 21. It was on the first floor, it developed, and a moment later he was knocking at the door. There was a noise from within, and then it opened. A tall, slim, blond young man was holding out his hand.

"Come in, Groody," he said, with the hint of a smile on his lips. "I'm Daly."

"Glad to know you," Groody said, as Daly shut the door behind him. "Not such a bad place to live, at that."

The walls of the room were stucco and the ceilings were high for the sake of coolness. A partition which did not reach the ceiling shielded the bathroom and through the doorless and curtainless opening in it Groody saw a modern shower bath outfit.

The telephone jangled on the wall.

"Excuse me just a minute," Daly said.

While he was discussing the matter of his laundry with the hotel clerk, Groody had a chance to scrutinize him more closely, and make up his mind that a somewhat astounding first impression became even more astonishing on closer inspection.

Daly was not as tall as Groody himself but he was still very close to six feet and almost as slender as Groody. His hair was blond and smoothly brushed and he was arrayed immaculately in white shirt and spotless white duck trousers and black and white shoes. His face was slightly tanned, although it did not approach the mahogany tint of Groody's own, and the features were so regular and perfect that he was entirely too good looking for a man. He looked like a twenty-two year old collar model. There was scarcely a line to indicate experience or character in that well-cut mask of a face, but all that it lacked seemed to have been concentrated in Daly's eyes.

Groody had been prepared, somewhat, for the appearance of his future confrere by the statement of Slim Evans that Daly's original face had been practically ruined in an airplane wreck, and that army plastic surgery had practically built him a new one. Nevertheless, as Daly turned from the telephone, there was what amounted to a definite physical shock when their eyes met. It was like looking down into the face of a little girl and seeing the eyes of an old woman who had suffered much.

THE DUKE'S EYES were blue-gray, set widely apart, but there was a sort of shadow in them. Set in that youthful face, they seemed to be the windows of the soul of a completely different person, as though the real Duke Daly was housed in an alien body.

"He's seen plenty, and gone through plenty, and he's been hurt bad," Groody thought instinctively. Aloud he said, "Well, Daly, I've heard considerable about you and I understand we're going to be hooked up in a little deal. Tom Service should be registering just about now, all dolled up like an international drummer, and he'll come sneaking down any minute. Think all these precautions were necessary?"

Daly nodded. He had scarcely smiled since Groody's entrance, and when he did there was no lightening in his eyes.

"Undoubtedly," he said. "The Von Sternberg secret service system is really remarkable."

"What's the exact lay at this moment, if anything?" Groody asked, tilting back his chair and taking out the inevitable cigar.

He was studying Daly steadily. Somehow his manner of speech and his choice of words did not seem to go with somebody who had been a part of the underworld between the ages of fifteen and twenty. That he was a special government agent now might explain that, though. A man could pick up plenty in ten years.

"I have made certain arrangements," Daly said, sitting down in a rocking chair and lighting a cigarette.

Groody felt himself being inspected so coolly and thoroughly that he seemed curiously like an insect under a microscope.

"Mr. Graves told you considerable about Von Sternberg, I presume, as well as the McMullen boys."

Groody nodded. He gave a quick resume of what he knew.

"All of which is accurate," Daly stated. "However, it goes even further than that, I believe, from what little I have been able to find out. I scarcely like to say what I believe to be the truth, and do not think I will. If you and Service come to the same conclusion, well and good, but I would hesitate to color your views with my theories and cause you to twist facts to suit theories."

HIS SPEECH WAS as precise as it was possible for speech to be and there was a curious evenness in his tones. They were uncolored with enthusiasm or interest of any sort, apparently.

"That's smart," nodded Groody. "If we got all hopped up on hearsay, everything we see we'd try to twist to fit it. This theory of yours makes the job any more difficult?"

"Not exactly," Daly said, "except that it would mean that Von Sternberg had many more allies and much more secret power than we had suspected heretofore. What I've arranged we'd better wait to go into until Service gets here."

"What's your own opinion of this Von Sternberg bozo?" Groody inquired, lifting one foot to the nearby table and sliding down on the back of his neck, as was his favorite posture. "Sounds like considerable of a man to me."

"'A poor benighted heathen, but a first class fighting man,'" quoted Daly, and the quotation did not escape Groody. "There is one psychological factor in him which colors everything he does, in my opinion, and which we should use for our own purposes. That's an overweening egotism, amounting to exhibitionism, if I make myself clear."

"Well, yes and no," grinned Groody. "In words of one syllable, he's considerable of a show-off, is that what you mean?"

"Exactly," Daly smiled and for the first time his eyes smiled with his lips. There was an amazing quick glow in them and at that second Duke Daly came alive to Groody. It was a brief flash of humanness which quickly disappeared. Had Groody known the Duke better, he would have realized that at that moment Daly had decided that he liked the sardonic newcomer.

"Exactly," he repeated. "He thinks of himself as a cross between the super-bandit of all times and the lone crusader. He would rather engineer a bizarre, theatrical and amazing coup which would set a million tongues to wagging, than do something ordinary which brought him in several times as much loot. For instance, one of his latest achievements. For what reason it was done, no one knows, except that the oil company concerned had offered a reward of ten thousand dollars for him dead or alive. The night following, Von Sternberg went to work. The company, the H. Wasta, had just about completed a new well in a new territory which had every sign of being a tremendous producer. There was a camp of seven or eight buildings and lots of machinery. The derrick was up and the well was down at least two thousand feet. There were probably a dozen men in the camp. The next morning the men, bound and gagged, were found piled like cord wood, although otherwise unharmed, and the derrick, machinery and entire camp had disappeared. The hole had been ruined and plugged up, and where the night before there had been a flourishing, lively camp, there was nothing—just the bare ground and a sort of little stump indicating where the well was being drilled. To add insult to injury, the president of the company found under the door of his house that same morning a courteous note from Von Sternberg enclosing ten pesos for an option on the machinery and material of the well."

Groody chuckled.

"I see what you mean," he nodded.

THAT'S HIS METHOD all the way along the line," Daly went on. "He's the kind that likes to warn somebody what he's going to do and then do it, despite them. The Mexicans, either openly or secretly, adore him. They call him *'El jinete de las Nubes.'* As you know, he operates only against Americans. Where his rendezvous is, or how many of them he has, no one knows. How many men he has right in Tampico, no one knows, and apparently his spies are everywhere. Sometimes a small army of his men do a trick on the ground. Other times airplanes are used. He's just a super-bush ranger, growing in power, influence and fame every day, and thumbing his nose at the world in general.

"His Border activities we know about, and the reason for them, but there is one thing to put down in our book. If and when we ever come to grips with him, remember that conceit and egotism of his. He's read Nietzsche until it's gone to his head, I guess, and all that Prussianism means—superman stuff and the haughtiness of the old nobility—is combined in him, plus the instinct of the actor. He pictures himself as a gentleman unafraid."

"I see," nodded Groody. "Well, as you say, we'd better wait until Tom gets here to go into details. I wonder if you'd mind if while we were waiting I took a shower. I've been on that boat so long, and it's so damned hot that it—"

"Surely," nodded Daly. "Hop to it."

In a moment Groody was behind the shower curtains luxuriating in tepid water which seemed to be affected by the enervating heat to the extent where it flowed with as little vigor as a Tampico resident moved.

He heard Service come in and shortly thereafter turned off the water. He had just reached around the curtain for a towel when there came another knock at the door.

"My laundry, I guess," he heard Daly say.

Daly went to the door and opened it.

"Buenos dias, señor," came a heavy voice. "May we enter?"

Some sixth sense caused Groody to freeze into immobility behind that curtain. As though in a dream he heard that same resonant bass say, "This is Mr. Daly, I believe? I am honored to meet you. Your friend I do not know. This is Mr. Johann Wolf, and I am the Count Friederich Von Sternberg."

7

GROODY STOOD THERE as if paralyzed.

"Won't you sit down?" he heard Daly say calmly, and then, utterly astonished as he was, he could not repress a grin as he heard Service say in his vacuous, hesitant way, "I'm g-glad to k-know you both. M-may I asked why you are c-calling?"

"You will pardon the intrusion, I trust," came that vibrant, heavy voice. Somehow it seemed to express limitless gusto and vitality. The famous bandit's words were carefully chosen, and while there was scarcely a hint of an accent, there was nevertheless the extreme care of a man who was trying methodically to speak a foreign tongue correctly. "You will pardon our guns? We do not intend to use them, I assure you."

Groody wrapped the towel around him silently as he heard the two men sit down.

"Good God, do you suppose he doesn't know I'm here?" he thought to himself. He glanced down. The curtain reached the floor and there was a good chance that he was absolutely invisible to Von Sternberg. He had undressed in the bathroom. "I don't see that there's any evidence of my having been here," he went on thinking. "Suppose I gave him the slip when I came in the room?"

"Well, Count Von Sternberg, I've heard much of you,"

Daly was saying. "I'm sorry that I'm not rich and have very little money about me. Aren't you sort of stepping out of your character?"

"You jest," came the count's voice. "It is my pleasure to have an understanding."

"By gorry, he doesn't know I'm here!" Groody thought exultantly, and yet he could think of no particular reason for exultation.

WHAT SPECIES OF freak was this Von Sternberg, running around Tampico when there was a reward on his head?

"I've been interested in you, Mr. Daly, since you arrived in Mexico," Von Sternberg went on meticulously, "and naturally I'm interested in your friends as well. You have been here long, Mr. Service, is it not?"

"N-no," Service said gently. "In f-fact I just arrived. W-why the guns, Count Von Sternberg?"

"You do not know me? You will permit me to doubt that."

It was then that Groody could repress his curiosity no longer. There within fifteen feet of him was the man they were after. Even were he discovered, there could be no harm done, and yet some sixth sense warned him that perhaps it would come in useful later if he were not discovered. With infinite care, as Von Sternberg was offering cigars in a courtly manner to Service and Daly, he inched the curtain apart and peered forth from his hiding place.

The man known as Wolf he could not see, but Von Sternberg was lighting Service's cigar for him in plain view. He was a giant of a man with thick blondish hair and a pair of shoulders like a wrestler's. He was dressed in spotless whipcord riding breeches and soft field boots and he wore no coat. His khaki colored silk shirt was immaculate and clung so tightly to his shoulders and torso that Groody could fairly see the muscles move.

The German had two guns swinging at his side in leather holsters, and the holsters were strapped down.

"Now we can talk in comfort," he was saying.

"As he turned toward his chair Groody got a look at his face. It was broad and square jawed and comely. Wide mouth, well cut nose, wide set glinting blue eyes below a broad forehead and thick hair, he was in a certain rugged way one of the most striking men Groody had ever seen.

"Would you be good enough to go out and get some beer, Johann?" he said as he was facing Groody, and his smile showed huge, white teeth.

There was a sort of electric vitality about him and he radiated strength and competence as a fire radiates heat, and yet already Groody could see in every move and word plain evidence of the fact that Von Sternberg was playing a part and enjoying it.

Johann left to carry out his chief's orders and Von Sternberg sat down.

GROODY ALLOWED THE curtains to come together again and stood as though turned to stone, straining his ears to hear what was being said. Were all their plans going to fall tumbling about their ears?

"It looks as though we were beaten before we started," he thought to himself.

"You say you've been interested in me," Daly asked him finally. "Why should The Cloud Rider—" somehow Groody sensed sarcasm in that title as Daly uttered it which evidently escaped the German—"be interested in me?"

"From certain facts in my possession," the Count said meticulously, "it occurred to me that perhaps you were interested in me."

"Well, that would be perfectly natural," Daly said calmly. "Isn't everybody interested in you? You don't seem to be very much worried, Count Von Sternberg, roaming around Tampico like this."

"I always know what I am doing," Von Sternberg said crisply. "Come, come, Mr. Daly, let us talk like men and not children. You are down here at the behest of the oil companies with whom I have been doing business, and your mission is to put me out of business, shall I say. Perhaps Mr. Service is here to help you."

"W-what gives you that idea?" Service asked mildly. "I knew Mr. Daly back in the States several years ago, and being d-down here and knowing he was here it w-was natural for me to l-look him up."

"Perhaps so. Perhaps not," Von Sternberg said. In every intonation of his resonant voice Groody could feel the enjoyment the outlaw was taking in the situation.

"Were that my purpose," Daly said with icy calm, "it would seem that you had put yourself in my power pretty thoroughly, Count Von Sternberg."

"Many people have thought that. You cannot blame me for wanting to talk matters over with a prospective competitor—no, that is the wrong word, a prospective obstacle in my path, shall we say. If I misjudge you and your purpose, I ask your pardon, but your conversation at the Colonial Club last evening with the four oil company men who have fought me most bitterly and least successfully, your frequent communications with the States, your careful inspection of the airdrome, airplanes and pilots who handle the transportation of the payrolls throughout the oil fields—"

"It occurs to me," Daly put in smoothly, "that maybe one Lieutenant O'Reilly has been telling you fairy tales."

Groody caught his breath. What madness had made the icy Daly say that.

FOR A SECOND there was absolute silence, and Groody was physically unable to prevent himself from parting the curtains slightly again to see what was happening. Von Sternberg was stooping down to pick up the cigar which he had apparently dropped.

"What do you know about Lieutenant O'Reilly?" he asked harshly. His lips were parted and there was nothing but wolfishness in his grimace. He sat there as though poised to spring.

Daly, lounging back easily, seemed entirely self-possessed. Service was polishing his glasses.

"Not a thing, personally," Daly said equably, his eyes on the outlaw. "However, Lieutenant O'Reilly did disappear, you know. Or perhaps you don't know. And two men were found killed in his ship on the Border a few days ago."

"Yes?" Von Sternberg said softly.

"Of course I know a few of the boys still," Daly went on, calm and cool as a glacier, "and I hear the gossip. Your old-time feud with O'Reilly is well known, naturally. Wouldn't it be natural for the boys to think you had something to do with his disappearance, and that very probably he's with you, either voluntarily or the reverse? The letter

I got was written only a couple of hours after they discovered that O'Reilly wasn't necessarily killed."

The Count settled back in his chair, and if Groody was any judge, he was a very thoughtful man.

"Whether my information comes from O'Reilly or not," Von Sternberg said carefully, "makes no difference. The fact that you know so much is additional proof of what I say."

"Pardon me, Count," Daly said smoothly, and with every word Groody was aware of an increasing admiration for Daly's outward calm. "I have nothing to conceal. I am a former flyer. I have a slight limp in my left leg, the result of an airplane accident. It was just enough to make me ineligible for further army flying, and for the last two years I have drifted around. I'm down here, true, to take a position as a pilot for the oil companies. In that capacity, should any attempt be made at a holdup, I should certainly try to interfere with the plans of the highwaymen—perhaps I should say skywaymen. That I admit. I trust you have no objection."

"It would be a pleasure to annoy you, sir," Count Von Sternberg said. "But be that as it may, I still insist we should talk like men. If the oil companies would only do that! How many times I have begged them! You would not believe it, but almost on my hands and knees I have begged them to pay me a suitable sum to make sure that they are not annoyed in the future. But a paltry quarter of a million dollars a year would be all that it would take to guarantee that they were not interfered with by any of the many criminals who infest the oil fields. That last statement is a sad fact, Mr. Service, but nevertheless a true one."

Groody's mouth widened.

"The old boy is certainly having himself a time," he thought.

WOLF CAME IN with the beer and Von Sternberg insisted on pouring it himself. A thousand mad schemes were swarming through Groody's mind. Could he, by some miracle bound out in the room and could the surprise of his entrance be used as a means to overcome the two self-confident outlaws? A dozen conceivable strategies occurred to him, but none seemed workable.

"Who knows how many allies he has hanging around the hotel, or maybe working right in the hotel," he thought. "He's sure of his ground or he wouldn't be here."

"Well, t-that's too bad," Service said gently. "It c-certainly is a t-tough life, isn't it, Count?"

"Ah, but very! Well, Mr. Daly, you will not be frank with me? Of course, I could go through your effects, sir, and doubtless gain more information concerning you. That I shall not do. We shall fight honorably, shall we not?"

"I don't get just what you mean," Daly told him.

"As you will," Von Sternberg said, and suddenly a new metallic note crept into his voice. He clipped off his words tersely and there was iron and ice in his tones as he went on. "I know why you are here, Mr. Daly. Doubtless you, also, Mr. Service. I have done myself the honor to call upon you to endeavor to dissuade you from causing yourself needless trouble. Before long you will realize who and what you are endeavoring to combat. Others more important and powerful than you, will also. I have warned you, sir. I have warned you both, if Mr. Service is your ally. What interests you represent, I do not know. I assume that there are resources behind you, even in the powerful government, may we say, but nevertheless, sir, you will do well to leave Tampico."

"I see no reason, Count Von Sternberg, for me to let you or anyone else interfere with my plans for making a living," Daly said calmly. "Suppose we say that I'll take my chances, go about my own business."

There was a click of Von Sternberg's heels on the floor as he got up.

"Very well, sir. And should we meet out over the monte we shall settle the matter," he said. "Now, gentlemen, there comes a peculiar problem."

His deep voice was lighted now and he was once again the debonair actor of a super role.

"I, of course, would not care to be troubled when I go out. Although I have some of my trusted men with me here and there, it could still be embarrassing. It would grieve me deeply to have to belittle you by tying you up. Would it not be much more comfortable and more sensible in every way for us to make a gentleman's agreement? Shall we declare an armistice for the next two hours, during which you not only give me your words of honor as gentlemen that you will make no attempt to start hostilities in any fashion but that none of the men under you, with you, or over you will take any steps against me? Shall we say that you promise me that no one will leave this room, telephone, or, otherwise communicate with the outside world for two hours?"

THERE WAS AN interval of tense silence. Then, "You hesitate. I, who hold the whip hand, extend to you a courtesy and you hesitate!"

"My word of honor, Count," came Daly's voice, "the

telephone will not be used, and neither Service nor myself will leave this room for two hours."

"Ah, but you choose your words!" the Count said and suddenly his voice was harsh. "I speak to you as a gentleman, sir. I ask from you the same spirit as is in me. I will not expect that you will seek loopholes in the terminology I employ. There will be no effort whatever on the part of you or any of your allies to make a move against me for two hours? It is an armistice for two hours during which your lips are sealed and your bodies as though in bonds."

"I agree, Count Von Sternberg," Daly said quietly, "and thank you for not tying us up."

"Damned if that doesn't let me out!" Groody thought. "Well, it saves me a trip down a strange corridor with nothing on but a towel, at that, probably."

"Until we meet again, then," came Von Sternberg's voice. "Two hours from now you can tell the story. Not so?" His slow, carefully chosen words, so meticulously pronounced, were curiously impressive. "Mr. Service, it has been a pleasure. Mr. Daly, my respects. Are you ready, Johann?"

The door closed behind them. Groody did not move. It was torture to stand there, but he wanted to take no chances. A thousand possibilities were in his mind, and above all it was physical torture to think of that audacious outlaw, a price on his head, the center of diplomatic argument, walking boldly down the hall of a hotel in the headquarters of his enemies.

As Daly went to the door and opened it Groody was thinking, "They said dead or alive. Well, I'll be damned if I'll ever see the day when I'll shoot that geezer in the back, or the front either, if I can help it."

"O.K., Groody," called Daly, and his voice had changed. There was a sort of excitement in it, and as Groody emerged from behind the curtains, his towel draped chastely around him, Duke Daly was a different person. His eyes were glowing, his face was slightly flushed, and behind his controlled movements there was an impression of jumping nerves held rigidly in check.

TOM SERVICE'S EYES were blazing through his glasses, as though he, too, sensed a climax which was near him.

"He never knew you were here," Daly said quietly, "which is a great break for us."

"Strikes me as though your head was right in a noose," Groody told him flatly. "And Tom's too. You two had better get the hell out of a country where an outlaw can do what he just did, because you haven't got a chance. Tom, maybe, yes, because he'll work on the ground, and has got a good alibi, but you—"

"Oh, to hell with that," Daly said impatiently. "I'll take a chance. Now listen. The scheme that I have cooked up with the oil men as a possibility is now the only thing to do. See what you think of it, Service. You, too, Groody. I believe the Count's grandstanding may play right into our hands, if we, mostly you, Groody, are willing to take a chance."

"I've been known to do that," Groody remarked casually, "but listen here. If he did get his information from O'Reilly, he knows about me, even though he hasn't seen me. And he's just as sure of Tom as he is of you."

"For some reason or another," Daly said, and it seemed as though a sort of tense quiet had descended on him, "I'm not so sure that he did get his information from O'Reilly. He never asked about you, and he didn't seem so sure of

Service. If he's had me followed closely, he could be reasonably sure of me. He's not infallible, you know, even though he thinks he is."

Groody nodded.

"Well, what is the scheme?" he asked. "We've got two hours to get it set."

"Well, even if it doesn't work, and even if he does know about you. I don't see where it can do any harm," Daly said levelly. "Nobody will be taking any more of a chance, as I see it, if Von Sternberg knows all about it, than they would if he doesn't. If O'Reilly has reached him and talked, it'll fail, and if we get hurt we'll at least have our eyes open. Now listen and see what you think of it."

They listened. Before it was over, Service, polishing his glasses, had forgotten his stuttering once more and talked as though every sentence was a separate spike driven into the structure he was building. Groody, sunk deep in his chair, with his long legs elevated to a table, threw in his suggestions, and Daly, tight lipped, and level voiced, talking as calmly as though he was discussing politics, helped move the plan. The contained government agent's eyes, though, Groody noticed, had come to life and the glow in them never died until the details were set.

8

ALL OF WHICH accounted for the fact that three days later Mr. Groody was sitting in the office of "Kid" Donovan, a stocky, hard-bitten oil man in the Querrara pumping station nearly a hundred miles from Tampico. Five miles away there was a primitive Mexican village, its houses located crazily with no thought for streets, and built of poles two or three inches apart and with thatched roofs. That was the only sign of civilization, if such it could be called, within twenty miles of the oil outpost in the middle of the monte.

"Well, George, about time we were startin'," said Donovan. "The tool pusher's outside."

Groody nodded.

"We'll see now whether we can get away with it," he stated calmly. "Before starting, I'll have another bottle of beer, if you don't mind."

Which he proceeded to enjoy with gusto. For the hundredth time he wondered just what his situation was. Not only had his mind been perpetually busy with the problem of Penoch O'Reilly, where he was and what he had told, but there were other things to be taken into consideration. He had been smuggled out of Tampico in the middle of the night and here at Querrara for the last two days he had lain very low, despite the fact that every man, down to the last laborer around the five wells and the pumping station, had been guaranteed loyal.

Querrara had been selected as a base by Daly and the oil men weeks before, and no stone had been left unturned to prevent Von Sternberg getting any inside information from any of its residents.

KID DONOVAN, WHOSE forty-five years sat lightly on his shoulders, had drilled for oil from Venezuela to Persia, and was one of the outstanding personalities of the whole oil business. Tough, competent, keen, able to do anything from drill a well to lay a pipe line, of his loyalty there could be no question. That he guaranteed personally every man in his little domain meant something. If Groody had succeeded in slipping into Tampico and then to Querrara without being suspected, and if Penoch O'Reilly had not succeeded in joining Von Sternberg up to the present—

"Oh, hell," Groody thought wearily, "why start figuring that all over again? The chances are ten to one that Von Sternberg knows everything that Penoch knows, or suspects, and the only grounds I've got for any hope whatever is the fact that Von Sternberg never mentioned me in Tampico. That might be just his method, though, fancying himself as a wise guy."

"Well," he said, glancing at his watch, "let's go."

The stocky, scarred faced oil man got to his feet. His overalls and shirt were spotted with oil and his heavy boots seemed soaked in it. What had once been a hat he perched on his curly head, and his blue eyes danced merrily.

"Wish I was going with you," he said. "I sure hope she works!"

They went out into the flooding sunshine and climbed

into the tool pusher which was no more nor less than a small, uncovered truck used to carry supplies around the field.

The office which was flanked by the bunk houses and the dining hall occupied an elevation from which Groody could survey the pumping station. It had been built to take care of the production of five wells and the station itself was set approximately in the middle of a circle the circumference of which would include those wells. There was an experimental dehydration plant set close to the pumping station and a dozen great sumps—basins dug in the ground to hold excess oil—formed a series of black lakes on every side of the pumping station. The ground was literally black with oil, and as Groody looked down at the layout it seemed that in the vicinity of the pumping station it would be impossible to walk because of the snarled mass of pipes.

There were pipes from the big storage tanks, pipes running from the sumps, pipes which carried the outflow of the pumps, and steam lines to the wells. It was a gaunt, unlovely scene, rimmed by the luxuriant jungle, but something about it seemed to express the raw gusto of the battle which was constantly being waged by the ambassadors of oil to wrest its riches from the earth.

As they climbed in the tool pusher, Jack Downs, a giant young Texan, came around the corner. He was in charge of the dehydration experiments in the plant down below the hill, and a man to tie to, if Groody was any judge. He was the only one in camp who knew definitely what Groody's plans were, and what he was there for. Downs pushed his sombrero back on his smooth black hair, and his broad, comely face lightened with a winning smile.

"Hop to it, big boy!" he chuckled. "If you have time, I wish you'd drop a bomb on that crazy professor of mine."

"The old doc been acting up again?"

"Hell, yes!" Downs said. "He's cuckoo. All inventors are, I guess. Well, you're going to try to take 'em, huh?"

"Those are my intentions," Groody stated, pushing his straw sombrero over his eyes.

"Well, good luck," Downs told him and Strode off toward the dining hall. He was a valiant trencherman.

THE TOOL PUSHER bounced along over a rough and winding road through the monte and Groody and Donovan talked casually. It was two o'clock in the afternoon and from the jungle there came a steady buzz of myriad insects. A deer vanished from the road as they rounded a turn, and thousands of brilliantly plumaged birds whirred among the branches of the trees.

The road was cut through the jungle, and finally it brought them by dint of many twists and turns to their goal. The protruding cap of an abandoned well—one of the many which Mexican rebels had ruined by leaving wide open years before until it had flowed itself out—was close to the side of the road. Set behind some trees were the buildings of the abandoned camp, and perhaps a quarter of a mile from the road was a huge, empty sump, its bottom almost as level as a floor.

"Back in 1919 or so this one was good for twenty thousand barrels a day," Donovan remarked to Groody. "Well, I guess everything's jake."

An old Mexican shambled into view from the trees

which partially screened the abandoned buildings. He had a long, grayish mustache, he limped slightly and he looked as though he'd been alive when Mexico was discovered. His face was a mass of wrinkles, but there peered forth from them a pair of dancing dark eyes which glowed with the light of perpetual youth. Manuel had been Donovan's faithful aid for more than ten years.

"Everything all right?" Donovan asked in Spanish as he steered the tool pusher across the rough ground toward the trees. Manuel had got on the running board.

"*Si, señor,*" smiled the old Mexican.

A moment later, the three men with Groody leading the way entered a crumbling shed. Within it, trim and glistening in its khaki paint, was the monoplane which Daly had labored stealthily for two weeks to hide so well that the world would be unaware of the fact that the ship was in existence. So far as anyone knew, there were but four men at Querrara, Donovan, Downs, Manuel and Groody himself, who had any idea that it was there, and only three in Tampico knew of it. From its shipment from the States to its final arrival there at the abandoned well, every care had been taken to keep its existence a secret.

Groody started the two hundred and fifty horse power radial motor in the shed. As it whispered along at idling, his eyes alternated between his instruments and his guns. There were two Brownings set in the center of the single wing, and there was a double Lewis on a scarf mount around the single cockpit.

"I'd call this being armed to the teeth," Groody remarked as he counted his ammunition drums and belts. "This, Donovan, if it interests you, is a ship!"

KING OF THE EXILES

HE HAD TO yell now above the noise of the motor as he increased its speed. His flyer's heart cherished every brace and spar and line of that last word in aircraft. From its single tapering wing to its short stream line fuselage it represented the highest point of speed, efficiency and economy which the aircraft industry had achieved, to his mind. One hundred and seventy miles an hour wide open, landing speed of less than forty miles, duralumin construction, all metal prop, an engine which faltered less often than the average automobile engine, it was in Groody's parlance "a honey."

"All set," he nodded. He wouldn't turn it all the way up in the shed, he decided.

With Manuel and Donovan guiding the wing tips, he taxied down to the sump. There Manuel put two stumps of logs under the wheels and for a few seconds the motor roared along wide open as the temperature gauge crept up to eighty degrees centigrade and the other needles shivered at the proper readings.

Groody glanced at the clock. It was time to go. A moment later the trim Beed had shot away like a runner from his mark and within fifty yards had taken the air. He did not circle the sump, nor look back at the men he had left behind him. Out over the limitless monte he sent the ship, keeping low for a while in an effort to avoid detection from any of the men at Querrara. Not until he was fifteen miles due west, did he lift the ship above an altitude of five hundred feet.

Still continuing his westward course he climbed the ship steeply until he reached eight thousand feet. He resembled a sort of Mephistopheles of the air with goggles and helmet on, and his narrow, sloping eyes swept the colorful monte below him ceaselessly. He could readily believe that nothing but a Mexican machete gang could even cut a pipe line through that tangled growth that he was looking down upon. Here and there were narrow *brechas* cut through it, and once in a while one of the hundreds of hidden pipe lines which the sweat of thousands of men had put through, was visible from his lofty perch.

Only part of his thoughts, however, were busy with the majestic and deadly scene below him. Had the trap been laid carefully enough? Fifteen miles ahead of him there came into view two clearings about three miles apart. Fifteen miles away to the south there was a small field. Here and there, as far as the eye could see, there were small breaks in the monte, most of which indicated the site of an abandoned well.

He strained his eyes northward as he banked his ship and circled widely. He had nothing to do but wait now. His timing had been correct almost to the dot. A speck took shape in the sky toward Tampico.

"There comes Duke Daly," Groody nodded. "I hope we're not on a wild goose chase."

He found himself tense with excitement now that that other plane had appeared in the sky and his eyes were strained forward almost continuously as he circled without cessation.

BY DOZENS OF underground channels in Tampico the word had been set in motion that very soon a huge sum of money in cash would be transported to Zacopatos to attend to the payrolls in that district without having to fly them weekly from Tampico. That it would be the first job of Duke Daly had been likewise gossiped about in certain quarters, if the propaganda had worked correctly. That Von Sternberg, who seemed to constantly have in his possession information which was far more secret than this rumor, would know about it, seemed a certainty. To make it additionally sure, one man, a *jefe* of a little settlement near Tampico who was suspected of being in active alliance with Von Sternberg, had been asked for a guard of soldiers at the take-off.

"That's all O.K.," Groody thought.

He was flying northward now as though to meet the other ship, but his course would carry him at least five miles east of Daly's, and as those two clearings down there made the only logical spot for a holdup between Tampico and Zacopatos, Von Sternberg would pick them if he was going to give them any action at all.

"By God, there they are!" he exclaimed. He picked up the powerful field glasses on the seat beside him to make sure. Two ships were flying from the west ten or twelve miles south of his position and probably fifteen miles west of it. He rocked his ship frantically, and then banked it. Then he straightened it out on a course which would intersect that of Daly's ship.

The Duke would have glasses, too, and he would have been searching steadily for the Von Sternberg ships, and must have seen them.

Within a minute and a half they had come close together, almost over one of the fields. Groody took a quick look at the little village so far to the south of him. There seemed to be no particular excitement down there. A few ant-like figures were visible around the huts, but that was all.

The other two ships were about ten miles away. Surely they would have glasses too. They would need them in their business if they were holdup ships.

Groody was above Daly and started into a dive. Daly zoomed up and banked. For a full thirty seconds the two ships indulged in a wild dog fight as Groody sent the monoplane twisting and turning through the air like a wild thing. When he was sure he could not possibly hit Daly, he fired his guns as well. Then Daly sent his ship into a tail spin. Groody followed it down, as the on-coming ships grew constantly in size.

RIGHT DOWN TO the clearing they went and Daly landed. Groody took time to circle once and fire a few shots from his front guns into the ground. There was little time to be lost now. He came down and landed alongside Daly. He hopped out of his ship, guns in hand just in case the pilots of the other ships had glasses, and Daly put his hands in the air.

"Hi, Duke!" Groody grinned as he bounded forward. His heart was pumping like mad and his eyes were flashing with a zest which indicated that this was one of the few moments of utter enjoyment which life had afforded him. His parachute in its bag was flapping around him but it scarcely seemed to impede his motion.

"Worked O.K.," Daly said levelly and his eyes were like pools of fire in his head. "Better work fast, Groody."

And Groody did. In a trice he had Daly's hands tied behind his back. He lifted a bag from the rear cockpit of the ship, slung it into his own, and took off in less than a minute. He barely cleared the monte on the edge of the clearing.

The other two ships had gone into a power dive now. They were about three miles away and were flashing toward the scene at close to two hundred miles an hour, as Groody straightened his plane. He flew due east, watching the oncoming ships constantly.

He was climbing speedily and was not trying as hard as he might have to elude pursuit. Nevertheless, if those pilots knew anything, they'd know that it was useless to chase him because he had at least a two-mile start on them and a faster ship.

He was three miles away as those two other ships circled the clearing, apparently scrutinizing the ship on the ground closely. Groody through the glasses, saw Daly turn and lean over as though to show the low-flying pilots that he was bound. One ship circled northward widely and came down for a landing.

Groody, literally afire, was still climbing steeply as he saw the man land. There could be no doubt in the minds of those other pilots that Daly's ship was one of the official oil company's ships.

"They're kind of puzzled, I imagine," Groody thought to himself exultantly. "Boy if we can only get away with this, and if the Count is only there himself!"

That was the catch. Was he? Perhaps it would be better if he were not.

Groody saw the other ship come down to land finally and now Daly would be explaining that he had been held up. Groody waited until the second ship had landed and its two puzzled occupants had alighted. There was only one man in the other ship. With the aid of the glasses Groody saw that Von Sternberg was not there.

Then he started to work. He was possibly eight miles north of Daly and the other pilots and three miles north of the second clearing. His hand on the throttle, he started to interfere with the even rhythm of his motor. He pulled the spark back to retard, jockeying with the altitude adjustment, and in a moment the radial motor was puffing and spitting as he turned the nose of his plane south and went into a glide for that other field.

Through his glasses he could see that the men on the ground were watching him continuously.

"Kind of surprised they've got competition in this holdup gag," Groody thought to himself. "I wonder if they can hear this."

HE SAW THE propellers of the ship start and he redoubled his efforts to make the motor sound like a stuttering and popping wreck. To all intents and purposes he was coming down for a forced landing.

He was low now and he saw them leap for their ships. Daly would have told them that he had the valuable cargo they were after in his ship and they were going to get it now.

"It's all according to Hoyle," Groody told himself.

His mouth was only a thin line now and that droop was far more pronounced. He took from underneath the seat a black cloth combination mask and helmet. He took off the leather helmet and pulled the other over his head. There were openings for eyes and nose, but otherwise his face and head were completely covered. He adjusted his goggles over the eyes and started maneuvering for his landing. If anything went wrong now, he was a gone gosling.

He was gliding in for a landing when the other ships

took the air. In single file they rose above the monte, pointed straight for the field which Groody was gliding into. Groody watched them carefully. They were both biplanes—Falcons, he thought. They would do about one hundred and forty miles an hour wide open. His ship could climb faster, fly faster and maneuver slightly better than theirs, but nevertheless they were two against one.

He played out the string to the limit. They were hurtling toward him, their undercarriages barely scraping the tops of the trees as he glided down into the field. He went so far as to touch his wheels to the ground, but at that moment the motor roared full on again, running sweetly and the Beed flashed across the ground and then barely cleared the barrier at the lower end as Groody lifted it in a mighty zoom.

Straight upward it traveled until it almost stood on its tail. He straightened it out, the motor wide open, and darted for the oncoming ships three hundred feet below him. Apparently the pilots didn't know what to do for the moment.

Now Daly had released the inefficiently tied bonds which held his wrists and was preparing to get under way himself. He would not join in the fray. That would be fatal. It would be illogical to the bandits. He was hemmed in by three enemies in their mind.

Before the outlaws could make up their mind, Groody was over them and had reached eight hundred feet. They were barely eight hundred feet high. He settled down to fly as a man who had got thirteen German planes in the war should.

He went up in a quick wingover and ended by pointing

straight at the lower ships. At that moment they started separating. His guns spoke. He did not want to kill them, but nevertheless he shot perilously close to the plane which had banked to the right. The Beed was darting downward at two hundred and fifty miles an hour as he pumped lead, first at ope ship and then at the other, striving to shoot only slightly over them and to one side of them.

ONE SHIP HAD a rear gun which the passenger worked, but Groody, snaking his Beed through the air like a darting dragonfly was careless of the shots. Then two bullet holes appeared in his right wing. In a trice he had sent his ship into a curving zoom which regained four hundred feet of altitude and the next second was pointing straight down for the single passenger ship.

Carefully he drew his bead as the ship with two passengers circled right to get a shot at him from below. He saw his tracers miss the twisting ship below by only about a foot and raised the nose of his plane slightly. Now they were pouring into the fuselage.

Suddenly the ship faltered. For a second it seemed to hang in the air and then fell off on a wing. An instant later a splotch of white billowed forth and the single pilot was swinging downward in a parachute directly over the second field. In a flash Groody twisted the Beed around and was pointed at the Falcon with two passengers in it.

It was below him and at his mercy. Again red spots danced before the muzzle of his gun as the Beed hurtled downward. Now the man in the back seat was standing up and waving a handkerchief. They were through and realized their helplessness.

It was here that Groody took his last desperate chance.

The Beed was three hundred feet higher than the lower ship and he nosed it all the way forward. The motor was full on and it traveled downward like a streak of light. He swayed it from side to side slightly, his eyes on the man in the back seat and ready for any emergency.

The Beed hurtled past the lower ship at nearly three hundred miles an hour and Groody pointed down toward the field below. He was ordering them to land.

The first ship had hit the ground and a huge ball of fire burst into being as the gas tank exploded. Obediently the other outlaw plane turned toward the field. The parachute jumper was landing and Groody sent the Beed roaring toward him. Three bursts into the ground warned the man below not to try to escape.

The rangy pilot was like some hawk-faced Nemesis as he circled the field watching the second ship land. He scribbled a note hastily and wrapped it around the wrench which he took from the tool kit.

"Get away from your ships and let me see plainly that you are unarmed. If there's any hesitating, I've got what it takes to cure you."

AFTER THEY LANDED he swooped low over the field and dropped the note. He saw them pick it up and read it and hold a hasty consultation. Then, as he circled around them he saw each of them throw two guns on the ground and walk slowly toward the edge of the field. They were evidently three very much puzzled and very much frightened men.

Groody brought his Beed in opposite them, taking every precaution and landing close to the monte on the eastern edge of the clearing to keep as far as possible from them.

Daly had taken off and was disappearing southward as would be natural for a lone payroll pilot in the middle of the monte.

Groody looked like some devil from the nether regions in his black mask and helmet as he swung his ship around until its nose was pointed toward his captives, but beneath that mask his mouth had widened in a saturnine grin and behind the goggles his narrow eyes were bright and cold.

He taxied almost squarely up to them, using his motor as a shield and then abruptly swung his ship to the right and had the men covered with the Lewises on the scarf mount. His right hand was on the trigger of the machinegun while his left one abstracted a cigar. He lifted the mask enough to put it in his mouth.

"Good afternoon, gentlemen," he said blithely. "It surely is going to be a pleasure to talk to you."

9

GROODY SURVEYED THEM leisurely as he lit a cigar. They were fifteen feet away from him and they were diversified types. One was tall and broad-shouldered and long-legged with a bold, harsh face and another one was a small young Mexican who somehow reminded Groody of a snake. The third man was really fat. His face was almost cherubic until one noticed the tiny eyes and pig-like nose. The tall man looked like a middle-aged Englishman, with his short clipped mustache and long face, and the fat one was as German as sauerkraut.

Groody was in his element, the more so because he knew that what happened in the next few minutes would be far more important than the mere shooting down of the bandits.

"Well, I see that our friend Von Sternberg didn't come with you," he said deliberately.

He unstrapped his belt and perched himself on top of the fuselage, his feet on the seat, but his hand never left his gun. The three men looked at each other silently.

"And who, may I awsk, are you?" the tall man said with an accent which removed all doubt of his British origin.

"Oh, I'm known as The Black Eagle," Groody said sardonically. "That's almost as flossy a title as The Cloud Rider. Is this what you boys were after?"

He held up the bag he had taken from Daly's ship, and that bag really did hold the equivalent of five thousand pesos. The beady-eyed little Mexican was looking at the ground. "Well, if we were, I should say you rawther spoiled our plans," the tall man said calmly.

"Think you're the only ones that know anything, huh?" Groody inquired. "Well, business has been so brisk for the Count that I thought I'd horn in."

All three of them were nervous and patently bewildered.

"Even so, may I awsk why you undertook to shoot us down? You could have escaped," the Englishman said. "Mind if I take off my helmet? It's beastly hot."

He removed his helmet and goggles, showing thin, sandy hair. His lantern jaw was covered with a stubble of beard, but even so he looked somehow immaculate in his riding breeches and boots and woolen shirt. That shirt was heavy and it was extremely hot, but he was apparently as cool as a cucumber.

"How could I know who you were? I wanted to make sure," Groody stated. "Suppose my engine went bad again?"

FOR A MOMENT there was silence. The fat German's face was a study of mingled bewilderment and resentment. He was scowling and his small mouth was pursed up in sort of a sullen pout. His hard, little eyes would not meet Groody's squarely, but the icy Englishman was suave and apparently untroubled. The Mexican looked as though he would have liked to have torn the mocking Groody limb from limb.

"I'll bet this Britisher heads the works in this particular deal," Groody thought to himself. "Those other guys are just toughs."

"Well," he said aloud, removing his cigar and holding the mask up so he could talk more clearly, "what's the boss going to say to you about this?"

"You seem sure that we have a boss," the Englishman said levelly. He was studying his lanky captor with a sort of cold appraisal which gave Groody the curious feeling that he could see through the mask he wore, even see through into his thoughts.

"Well, boss or no boss, I don't know what to do with you," Groody said lightly. "I naturally assumed that you were part of Von Sternberg's mob, they being pretty famous around here. I've been trying to get to that bozo for a long time. That was one of the reasons I invited you to this little tea party, as it were."

The German and the Mexican looked at each other and the lantern-jawed Englishman's cool blue eyes seemed to become more piercing. He scratched his long, slightly crooked nose reflectively.

"Would you mind repeating that?" he asked.

"No. I thought maybe he and I could do some business if I could ever get to him," Groody said in a casual voice.

There was a moment's silence broken only by the drone of the insects and the soft whisper of Groody's idling motor which was barely discernible as the prop turned lazily.

Groody was sweating below his mask, but he did not think the time ripe to take it off as yet. He had a part to play.

"I don't quite understand."

"Well, then, I'll draw a map of it," Groody told him. "I'm down here to get some jack, as you've seen for yourself. This Von Sternberg seems to have the industry pretty well sewed up, so to speak. I wouldn't mind throwing in with him if the proposition was right and he needed a good man. And I *am* a good man—in the air or on the ground!" he added harshly.

THE GERMAN'S EYES seemed to have become smaller, as though the flesh had gathered more closely around them, and the little Mexican was looking on as though he could not believe his ears. He was a sleek, olive-skinned young fellow with a rat-like quality in his face. Groody wouldn't have trusted him as far as he could have thrown his airplane.

Not a word was spoken by the outlaws. The Englishman seemed immersed in thought, but his prominent blue eyes seemed to bulge a little more, as though he were making a strenuous effort to probe into the mental processes of the masked man before him.

"Oh, come on! Let's get together, now," Groody said suddenly. "I've just got an idea in my mind. If I'm willing to take a chance, you ought to be. In fact, you're not taking any chance at all. I know you're Von Sternberg's men. Let's not beat the devil around the stump. I'll tell you what I'm willing to do for an interview with him, now that I come to think of it. I'm getting tired of horsing around as a lone wolf and I want some real action with some real guys. Shouldn't be any objection to me introducing myself to your mob by throwing in this bagful of change I slipped away from you there, a damned good ship and three of his own gang along with me, should there?"

"Just what do you mean?" the Englishman said in a deliberate, cool voice.

The Mexican's eyes were suddenly shining and he was wetting his lips as though he could scarcely believe his ears.

"I'm making a proposition to throw in with you," Groody said flatly. "In his racket he can always use men like you and me. I don't know yet how much is in this bag, but there's dough in it. I don't believe it's as much as I figured it would be, at that, but I'm willing to follow you guys back to where you came from and let you carry this money. I'll throw it into the kitty and you can come back with the dough you went after and a new recruit. You've got everything to gain and nothing to lose. If I'm not on the level, where am I? All alone in the midst of a strange mob who can do anything from shoot me to keep a ball and chain on me and make me cook for 'em.

"On the other hand, I can take off with this coin, break up your ship for you, leave you out here and see to it that you're captured, as far as that's concerned. What about it?"

Again that silence followed. The Mexican and the German looked at their tall companion, and then and there any doubt as to who was most important among the trio was washed away.

"I'll bet he's a big guy in the main mob, too," Groody thought to himself. "There's a bozo to cultivate."

Casually he lifted his hand and took off that mask and helmet. As the bold outlines of his aquiline face came into view the three men seemed to stare at it as though fascinated.

"Well, I can't wait all afternoon," Groody said suddenly, and there was a harder note in his voice. "I've made you a proposition. If you're Von Sternberg men, I want to see him because I'm looking for the right kind of a mob to work with. Make up your mind, buddies, and make it up quick."

He was talking purposely in the vernacular to carry out his pose of being a badman.

"My cards are on the table. I'm taking a chance on being ambushed, and I'm giving you the money, but I'm doing it because I know damned well that Von Sternberg can use me and that I can use him. Speak quick, or I'm off."

THE MEXICAN BROKE into a quick flow of liquid Spanish, the German nodded and the Englishman was stroking his mustache thoughtfully. Then suddenly he raised his eyes to Groody's.

"I will take it upon myself to do it," he said with that icy calm. His cadaverous face was spread with a sort of pallor now, showing red spots in each hollow cheek. "That is, sir, to this extent. I shall arrange an interview with the man you wish to see—"

The German interrupted him, and this time he talked German. It was a guttural flow of speech accompanied with jerky gestures.

"It has been suggested," the Englishman said finally, "that my plan is unnecessary. We think—"

"Oh, to hell with what you think!" Groody said with sudden carefully calculated savagery. That Englishman was a game bird, Groody was thinking. He dropped down into his cockpit. "Now you three are going to do what I say, or I'll blow every one of you to kingdom come. You, tall boy, do it. Take off your belt and just temporarily tie this little Mex's hands behind his back, and I want it done right, understand?"

The Englishman hesitated.

"Come on! Snap into it!" Groody yelled harshly, and without a word the Englishman did it. The Mexican was like a cornered rat, wetting his lips with his tongue incessantly.

"Now that shirt of yours will do very well to do the same for the Dutchman," Groody snapped.

It was done under Groody's critical eyes.

"Now back up here to this ship yourself."

He took some safety wire from his kit and started to bind the Englishman when that contained outlaw asked quietly, "What is it your intention to do, may I awsk?"

"Disarm your ship and then force you to guide me to Von Sternberg," Groody told him flatly. "I'll be damned if I'm going to let a lot of underlings stop me from what I want to do. You haven't got guts enough or brains enough between you to know a good thing when you see it. If the rest of Von Sternberg's mob is like you three, it's not going to take me more than one day to be the crown prince, so to speak. You'll either guide me there, or you'll be shot down like so many pigeons, understand?"

He got out of the ship, Colt in hand and herded them over toward their own craft. The guns were modern, he saw duplicates of his own, and it took but a moment to remove all the ammunition beneath the eyes of the quiet outlaws.

"All right, gentlemen," he said, after it was safely disposed of. "Now you can take off and I'll give you just one break. You—by the way, what's your name?" He was speaking to the Englishman.

"Is that material?" was the equable answer.

It seemed as though the tall outlaw's eyes could not

leave Groody, and it was as plain to the airman as anything could be that the Britisher was grappling mentally with the problem which had been presented to him. He was not yet convinced that he would be justified in aiding and abetting Groody in reaching Von Sternberg.

"Well, maybe it isn't material," barked Groody, "but just because I'm soft-hearted and tender by nature I'm going to give you one break. I don't aim to be a good shot unless I have to be. If you lead me to Von Sternberg, I'll take my own chances, and your chief'll never know from me, unless I have to tell him what humiliating circumstances you three brought me in. The day will come and come very soon when the fact that you hesitated and made me force you to do it will get you laughed at plenty. I'm going to mean more to you and the whole mob than forty payrolls, you mark my words."

He was playing his part to the hilt, endeavoring to impress himself upon them as hard and reckless and superbly self-confident. He unbound the quiet Englishman quickly. He was back at his machine-gun now and had no fear of treachery.

"Now unbind your friends, get in that ship, and just one last word. A false move out of you, and you're through, and don't forget this. I saw where you flew from and I've not been batting around Mexico this long without having a pretty accurate idea of where I'm going. Now get these instructions, and get them right."

"You need to give us none," the Englishman said unexpectedly.

"No?" barked Groody. "How to me?"

"I have made up my mind. James is my name, sir, Albert

James. I shall lead you to where you want to go, and I give you my word that you need have no fear so long as you conduct yourself as you should."

And the funny part of it was, as Groody thought afterward, he said that as though he really believed his word of some value.

10

NEARLY TEN THOUSAND feet high, the powerful motor throttled slightly to keep behind the bandits' plane, Groody indulged in a great deal of thinking as the two ships droned their way westward.

Gradually the luxuriance of the jungle changed. The low foothills merged into steeper slopes and the tangled *chijol,* ebony and *ceron* trees, interspersed with palms and *choca,* changed almost imperceptibly into gnarled chaparral.

The earth, which was so rich that the peon could drive a stick through it, plant corn and forget it until the corn was harvested, seemed to change into barren soil that was incapable of producing anything but cactus, sagebrush and mesquite.

The hills ahead seemed to indicate that they were the repository for many a sinister secret, and their rugged outlines brought back more forcefully to Groody the number of potentialities of the dilemma that might be facing him. It was surprising that James had hesitated so long in accepting his offer Even though the lanky Englishman were certain that Groody did not mean all he said, the fact that he was following them to some unknown rendezvous did not mean at all that he was safe, or anywhere near it. Despite the fact that he had tried to foresee every possible complication, the hawk-faced pilot knew that he was sitting on a volcano.

IF PENOCH O'REILLY was a voluntary member of Von Sternberg's band, the jig was probably up. There was just a chance in that event that he could convince even O'Reilly that he had turned traitor to the task which had been set him, but it was a slim one. Even were O'Reilly not there, Von Sternberg, with all his facilities for gaining information, might know just as much about him as he apparently did about Daly. The very fact that James, who seemed to carry considerable weight in the Von Sternberg organization, had hesitated as long as he had, seemed to indicate that something was known about Groody's presence in Mexico. Otherwise why would he have hesitated? There was money, and a marvelous ship in perfect condition to be added to the bandits' store, even though they killed Groody himself or kept him captive because they had no confidence in him. No matter how reckless or desperate Groody might have been, he was still a lamb going into a den of wolves, without a chance if they decided to disbelieve him or if they knew that he was not what he pretended to be.

His lean face set in harder lines as his ship skimmed over the top of a mountain, and, veteran as he was of a thousand tight spots in most of the corners of the world, he was aware of the fact that he had never thrust his head into an unknown lion's mouth as he was doing now. However, there was something about that long flight over the barren desolation below, with God alone knew what ahead of him, which called to every instinct within him.

As the years had gone by and the careless, devil-may-care twenties had merged into the harder and more reckless thirties, one characteristic had grown in the lanky pilot until it had come to be the strongest single force in his life. His annoying restlessness and discontent was only completely assuaged, and then only temporarily, by intervals like this, so tense and so pregnant with possibilities that all discontent was forgotten and he could live in the zestful moment.

So it was that winging his way through the tranquil sky, toward the sun which was almost ready to touch the rim of the horizon, George Groody's heart was in his mouth, but his spirit was content.

Steadily the Falcon ahead of him drove onward over a desolate little valley toward the side of rugged peaks ahead. They had come more than one hundred and fifty miles from the scene of the holdup, for nearly an hour not a sign of even primitive life had Groody seen. Surely Von Sternberg could not operate continuously from this distance, he was thinking. Was he being led into a trap?

Three minutes later the Beed hurtled itself over the crest of the mountain ahead and Groody's sloping eyes stared down at the ground fascinatedly. A little stream ran through a valley which was scarcely a mile wide, and it was like coming on a little oasis in the middle of the desert. There were some cultivated fields, surrounded by little splotches of monte which seemed allied with that fifty miles back of them, and at the upper end of the valley, surrounded on three sides by hills, there was a thatched roof settlement. A gorge ran back into the mountain at the north and it was from this that the stream seemed to proceed.

HALF THE WAY down the valley there was a long, narrow

field, skirting the eastern slope, and half way down the length of it there was what seemed like the mouth of a cave at least a hundred yards wide. Farther on down the valley there was another little settlement. The huts seemed to be made of adobe there, and the whole appearance of it was different from the half camp, half settlement on the northern end of the valley.

Now he picked up several other things of interest as he saw the bandit ship start into a dive. One of them was what seemed like a shed at the northern end of that long, narrow field, and another was that there were a considerable number of cattle grazing here and there through the valley. There were horses, too, and as he came lower, following the other ship down, he saw that they were good horses.

On the tops of the mountains immediately surrounding the more northerly settlement he saw three little shacks, now, and close to each one of them there was a man. Looking more closely, he saw that each man had a pair of glasses to his eyes. The one on the east drew a gun and Groody saw him shoot it in to the air several times, evidently as a signal to those below.

Now, as he spiraled down back of James, he saw signs of intense activity. Three men popped out from the broad mouth of that hollow in the side of the mountain into the field, and from the huts in the northern settlement there came several men. Two of them mounted horses and started galloping for the field.

"Strikes me as though this was the corral of the said Cloud Rider," Groody thought to himself, and every nerve in his body started to jump. He was aware of a slight, not unpleasant, breathlessness, and his jaw set as though in anticipation of the struggle to come.

Holding his nose, he blew out his ears to compensate for the quick change in altitude and followed James down like a hound on the trail. The bandit ship circled southward over the open field and started in for its landing. Groody, eager to dispel suspicion, stayed as close to James as he could and was just as low.

Close to the southern boundary of the smooth, specially constructed field, he banked around, waiting for James to land. The bandit ship landed smoothly and then Groody started down. He did not bother to circle back for a long glide in as James had. Partially because it was his bent and partially to impress himself on the spectators below, he started his landing one hundred and fifty feet high and barely fifty feet back of the boundary.

As he banked around, his ship was pointed at the mountain close by and at right angles to the field. He tipped it up in a vertical bank and jammed on full top rudder. He sent his ship almost straight downward in a vertical side slip. Fifty feet above the ground and still only fifty feet from the boundary, he brought it out facing the field, only to bank to the right, then to the left and side slip further. **AGAIN HE STRAIGHTENED** it barely fifteen feet above the ground and as it rushed for the fence he gave it full right rudder, skidding tremendously to kill his speed. He landed lightly fifty feet from the fence. The whole thing was the result of perfect control of his ship and utter self-confidence. Groody was born for the air.

James had taxied to the very mouth of the cave and the three bandits had piled out of the ship and were talking excitedly to the three waiting men. Groody taxied up slowly, looking them over. Two of them were Mexicans, each with a machete at his side and a gun at his hip. The third man was a slender, fox-faced redheaded young fellow who looked like an American. He had a cap on his head, pulled slightly over one eye, which seemed as incongruous in that setting as a high silk would have.

The two horsemen were galloping across the field now, and Groody noticed that they rode very good horses.

He unstrapped his parachute and climbed out as nonchalantly as he could. The remnant of an unlit cigar was still in his mouth, and he proceeded to light it as he lounged over toward the group of men with his customary bent-kneed stride.

James took a few steps forward to meet him, and his bulging eyes seemed a trifle more friendly, somehow.

"Sort of a long hop, eh, what?" he said calmly. "Meet Wildcat Williams, one of your countrymen."

The little redhead came forward. He was dressed in cowboy boots and his legs were slightly bowed. Very light, cold eyes surveyed Groody without expression.

"By the way, I don't know your name," James said.

"Dooly," Groody told him, "and just in order to be in the running with the Wildcat here, I'll state that the nickname is Eaglebeak. Not so pretty as Wildcat, but deserved, I presume. I'm glad to know you, Williams."

He stood there quietly, looking down into the eyes of the terrier-like little man before him. If ever he had felt instinctively that he was in the presence of a cold blooded killer, it was when he looked down at Williams. He had not offered to shake hands until Williams had thrust out his own.

"Pleased to meet you," the little redhead said with a slow Texas drawl. "You came in sudden like, didn't you?"

Groody nodded, as the two horsemen galloped up. He did not even turn his head to look at them for the moment.

"Saw my chance and took it. Hope you boys are satisfied to put your brand on me.

He turned around as Williams took out a plug of tobacco without answering, and confronted two faces which expressed a mixture of bewilderment and suspicion. One was a stout Mexican whose fleshy face was garnished with a luxuriant black mustache. His beauty was not increased by a great many pock marks, but nevertheless there was something impressive in his big black eyes, bushy black eyebrows and square shoulders. He was dressed with considerable ostentation in full Mexican regalia, heavily studded with silver lace. His black sombrero was surrounded with a band of twisted silver and leather, which looked like a load in itself for a man to carry.

James talked to them in Spanish.

THE SECOND MAN, his eyes never leaving Groody, swung down off his horse as James talked calmly. The Mexican just sat there, stroking his mustache. The man who had dismounted rolled a cigarette with practiced ease, and it was his appraisal which Groody returned with the most interest.

In the first place he was very young, apparently not over twenty-six or seven, and never had Groody seen such utter recklessness and carefree abandon expressed in a man's countenance in his life. He had crisp, slightly curly hair of a peculiar shade between brown and gold, a sort of burnished bronze, and it was trimmed so neatly and parted so exactly that Groody's thought was, "I wonder if they've got a barber shop in this outfit." His eyes were slightly oriental in that they were a bit narrow and seemed to slant just a trifle upward and outward. They were a curious hazel color and the whites were so clear that in contrast to his deeply tanned countenance they were almost startling. His nose was well shaped but did not jut very far forward from his face. It seemed to protrude from his eyes and then curve almost straight downward. The nostrils were very thin above a wide mouth which had more twists in it than Groody's own. It seemed to be set slightly slantwise, giving the lower part of his face a rather one-sided expression, and below it his jaw was thin and square.

As he listened to James a smile played about his lips, and when his eyes met Groody's it seemed that there was a careless laugh in them. It was as though the young fellow was saying, "Well, who gives a damn who or what he is? We don't care."

He was dressed in boots and stained khaki riding breeches, and his gray flannel shirt was open at the neck, its collar resting casually in a cross between standing up and laying down. Perched on the back of his head was a stained gray sombrero, the brim of which came to a point in front and was deeply rolled.

Groody's practiced eyes noted that there was a shoulder holster below the loosely fitting shirt, under the left arm. As he smoked his cigarette his arms were loosely crossed, and his right hand, Groody noticed, was playing with the flap of his shirt, as though he liked to have it close to his gun.

The Mexican asked two questions in Spanish and seemed to be expostulating with James. The sandy Englishman stood his ground without heat. Suddenly the younger man interrupted the colloquy with careless impudence.

"Oh, what the hell," he said. "It's the chief's business anyway. Got to give a man credit for having some brains."

His speech was couched in soft tones which did not smack of Texas to Groody but rather of Mississippi or Louisiana. He lounged forward slowly, as though there was no energy in him.

"Hello, Mr. Dooly," he grinned, "and many thanks for the ship and that *dinero*. James has been telling me about it."

GROODY SHOOK HANDS and grinned down at him sardonically. He was not fooled by those smiling eyes and that mouth which widened into an apparently frank smile. Perhaps the young fellow before him was a gambler, but of all the men that Groody had seen, the Southerner was the last one he would pick to ring in a phony deck on him. He had an idea that the loose-jointed young fellow before him would strike with approximately the speed of a rattlesnake.

"Your name being what?" Groody inquired.

"They call me the Cactus Kid around here, having a weakness for nicknames," grinned the other. "Right names don't matter such a hell of a lot, do they?"

"And this is General Lopez," Jambs told Groody, and the Mexican lifted his hat, his heavy face unchanging.

"Where do I get my credentials, if I get any?"

By now several Mexicans who had been working in

the fields or doing odd jobs had gathered close to them and were surveying the newcomer and talking with many gesticulations.

"We'll go up and see the chief," the Cactus Kid said, and it struck Groody that the young fellow was very sure of himself. "Come on, m'lord."

This last remark was to James. Groody was to find out later that the Cactus Kid delighted in taking pot shots at the pallid Englishman with great frequency.

"I'll lead my horse, Lopez," the Southerner said carelessly. "You might ride ahead and tell the chief we're coming."

The Mexican nodded and set off at a mad gallop for the little settlement.

NOW WHAT THE hell are you doing here?" came that creamy drawl.

"Oh, the same thing as you are, let's say," Groody told him as they walked along. "I told James here enough, and I'll tell the rest to the boss, I guess."

The Southerner looked around quickly and sudden resentment seemed to shine through his startling eyes. Groody, his eyes heavy lidded, and that sweeping line very deep around his mouth, stared back without giving an inch, and there was something stark and steel-like in his aquiline face at the moment. This was no time to be buffaloed.

"So that's what you think of yourself," the Southerner drawled thoughtfully, and apparently his quick resentment had passed. "Don't fancy yourself as a big shot, by any chance, do you?"

"Not a bit of it," Groody told him levelly. "I'm taking all the chances on this deal and I'll throw in my share if I'm in. On the other hand, I don't want to be anywhere I'm not wanted."

"How do you think you're going to get out, just in case you're not? We're pretty exclusive around here."

"I know all about you, or I wouldn't be here," Groody told him, "and I don't aim to be scared of all this artillery any more than I need it proved to me that you're tough guys, understand?"

Again their eyes met and suddenly the devil-may-care Southerner grinned.

"Well, we'll see about that," he said.

Half a dozen Mexicans stared at them curiously as they walked down the short street. Groody noted that the little settlement was laid out with military exactness, in great contrast to the ordinary primitive Mexican town in the bush. Everything was spotlessly clean, and the short streets were not only laid out with military precision, but had been cleared of every vestige of vegetation. The walls of the huts were made of *choca*, a tree which when cut from its stump will grow if thrust into the ground again and there were no interstices between the poles.

Then he caught sight of a building hidden behind chaparral on the side of the mountain at the upper end of the short street. It was a frame affair and he saw such things as a screened porch, and then noted for the first time that the town was electrically lighted.

"No doubt in the world," he thought to himself, "that this is G.H.Q."

James said nothing and the Cactus Kid seemed immersed in thought. As they approached the half hidden house, three or four men who might have been German,

English or American came down the steps, and as they passed Groody and the others stared interestedly, but did not say a word.

"How many flyers in the outfit?" he inquired casually.

"You'll find that out later, maybe," the Southerner told him.

"Just wanted to know whether there was room for another one," he told him spaciously as he threw away the stump of his cigar and took out another one. "Good God, what are you guys scared of?"

"Don't flatter yourself," drawled the Southerner. "It takes a reputation to work for the chief."

"Yeah? I don't see anything so all-fired attractive about it," Groody stated, "as worked at present. If I didn't figure on bigger stuff happening, I wouldn't be here."

"Huh?"

IT WAS A surprised grunt from the placid Southerner and suddenly his oriental looking eyes were very keen and hard.

"Just what are you getting at, stranger?"

"Nothing special," Groody told him calmly, but nevertheless he knew that he had jolted the Cactus Kid out of his calm. "Just strikes me as though there is many a point the chief has missed for real dough. Now take the Border stuff, for instance. Good God, he's nuts on that! Why it looks to me, the way he's sitting, he could go for millions."

He hesitated a moment, and then took a chance. They were close to the steps now.

"And it was my understanding," he went on deliberately, "that that's what he's planning. That's why I'm here."

The Southerner's gaze was level and thoughtful and his eyes seemed wider, as though he was struggling between two emotions, consuming interest and suspicion. Then he seemed to relax as they reached the steps.

"Well, you better have your pedigree all wrote out," he said. Somehow that soft drawl made his grammatical errors attractive rather than the reverse, and his dropped g's and slurred speech fell pleasantly on the ear.

They went up the steps after the Cactus Kid ranged his horse alongside General Lopez's, and Groody confronted the gaze of two more Mexicans who were sitting behind the screen. One was tall and slim and dandified with a pointed mustache and a vulture-like face, and the other one was a handsome man of about thirty-two, Whose attire, if anything, outshone that of Lopez. They gazed at him without particular interest, and the thin one, whose looks Groody did not like, said something in Spanish to his companion, which made them both laugh. It was as though he was being looked at as a prospective sacrifice. In any event it was plain that they were neither worried nor particularly interested because of his presence.

"I shall see whether he will see you now," James said calmly. "Come inside."

Groody entered a shadowy room which was bare save for a desk, one chair which was occupied by a young German with blond hair and mustache, and a cabinet which Groody had to look at twice to believe his own eyes. There was no doubt about it. It was a radio sending and receiving set.

"Will the chief see Mr. Dooly?" James asked the young German.

The man behind the desk pulled at his crooked nose which had apparently been broken, and looked at Groody with a sort of empty look in his close-set, China blue eyes.

"I vill see," he said with a strong German accent.

He disappeared through a door which opened into a passage, and which he closed carefully behind him.

"Plenty of ceremony, I should say," Groody remarked sardonically. "Runs this like the Army, eh?"

"Well, see you later," the Cactus Kid said blithely. "I'm going out with those spigs and have a drink."

HE SEEMED TO have a careless contempt for everything and everybody around the place, Groody reflected, and his interest in the remarkable looking Southerner had not stopped increasing yet. The German appeared through the door. "You vill have to vait a few minutes," he said.

The few minutes grew to twenty and not a word was spoken. James seemed preoccupied with his thoughts and Groody reposed himself restfully sitting down against the wall, despite the black looks of the young German who was busy with some figures. It was as though he resented the immaculate barrenness of his office being spoiled by such unconventional behavior.

Finally a little bell rang and he disappeared.

"You vill go in," he said, when he reappeared. "You, too, Mr. James."

A moment later Groody, unconsciously squaring his shoulders to meet the ordeal, stepped through the door at the lower end of the passage ahead of James to face the man who might know him and all about him.

11

VON STERNBERG WAS seated behind a huge desk and as Groody stepped in the doorway he was subconsciously aware that the big room was furnished in a riot of color. Indian blankets were on the walls, bright colored rugs on the floors, an electric fan buzzed busily in one corner and there was a couch which held many sofa cushions of many hues. There were three or four chairs, all of them large and comfortable, and the row of buttons there on the desk would have done credit to a city executive.

The huge German simply sat there, and Groody stood quietly returning the gaze of Von Sternberg's piercing eyes. They were as long and narrow as Groody's own but they ran straight across his face below blond eyebrows which were like lines ruled off on his forehead, paralleling his eyes. His thick, blond pompadour grew close to his head and was cut off straight on top, giving his countenance the impression of absolute squareness.

For at least thirty seconds the outlaw maintained silence and James did not break it.

"So," Von Sternberg said finally, "We have a visitor. Not so? Will you permit me to compliment you on your courage, Mr. Dooly?"

Groody had figured out in advance from his slight knowledge of Von Sternberg how he should act. He must make no mistakes, and he was up against a different proposition now than he had been with Von Sternberg's subordinates.

"Great rewards," he said calmly, "sometimes require great risks."

"You wish to be one of us, I am told," Von Sternberg said, continuing that impassive scrutiny of the rangy airman before him.

"I do," Groody said promptly.

"Why?"

"I think there's more in it for me, and from all I hear about you, you are my kind of a man."

Von Sternberg's lips parted in a wolfish sort of smile.

"Which does not mean that you are my kind of a man," he said.

HE WAS PLAYING another part now, Groody saw. His body was as immobile as though he was a statue. Not a finger moved. Big and blond and quiet, he merely sat there, monarch of all he surveyed.

"I think I am," Groody said quietly.

"Words are cheap. Who are you, and where do you come from?"

"That's neither here nor there," Groody told him levelly. "Perhaps if I wanted to tell you all that, I wouldn't be here."

For a few seconds Von Sternberg studied him, from his bold face to his negligent, bent-kneed posture. Then his eyes shifted to the quiet Englishman.

"How did this happen?" he snapped gutturally, and Groody thought, "No wonder those bozos weren't so happy at the idea of coming back without the ship and without the money."

James, to Groody's surprise, went into German, of which Groody had a smattering as the result of his years of the War. Quietly and unemotionally James told the story and so far as Groody could gather, told it exactly. Was Von Sternberg playing with him, as a cat would a mouse? Not a word had been spoken to indicate that he was suspicious or that he knew anything concerning Groody, but there had been something about that grin which was like a lion licking its chops at the prospect of a juicy morsel.

"So," Von Sternberg said slowly, when James had ceased. His body did not move, but his eyes switched to Groody. "You are American. You learned to fly in the American Army, not so?"

"I refuse to answer any questions whatever about myself," Groody said steadily. "I merely came here with a good ship and several thousand dollars to throw into the pot and am asking for a job, and I don't mean an ordinary job, either."

"No?" Von Sternberg said, and suddenly his face seemed to be slightly more animated and the magnetism of the man to shine through his motionless body. "You mean just what?"

"I mean I'm not going to be a flunky around here," Groody declared. "Not that I expect to be the boss, but I'm not going to be a buck private in the rear rank, either."

"You would be exactly what I wish," Von Sternberg said, his big white teeth showing slightly. He was studying Groody with more interest now. "Just what do you think you could do for me, even if I should allow you to do it?"

"Well, for one thing," Groody said, "I'll outfly anybody in your mob and take more chances and get away with more stuff, and you can call that any time you want to."

Suddenly Von Sternberg's eyes were alive with interest and for the first time he moved.

"You speak big words," he said, and his smile lighted up his square face amazingly.

"Furthermore," Groody went on, "I'm here because it's in the wind that you're up to bigger things than you ever were in the past."

Von Sternberg's eyes widened.

"Yes?" he said harshly, and his huge body bent forward over the desk as though he was about to spring from his chair. "You have been hearing fairy tales."

GROODY GRINNED, AND despite himself there was a saturnine quality about him, as he said seriously, "Perhaps so, but the name of Von Sternberg is on every tongue. You know that."

"Perhaps people exaggerate."

Von Sternberg relaxed slightly.

"You think you could help *me* accomplish bigger things," he said, giving an effect of god-like amusement at the foolishness of a child.

"I know damn well I could," Groody told him flatly. "I'm no amateur, you know, Count. I'm interested in big stuff to be sure, but even those payroll jobs and all that, I can do a lot better for you than a lot of people."

"Yes? How?"

"Well, for one thing," Groody told him, aware all the time of the examination he was undergoing, "you're not going to be able to operate much longer. The way you work it you've got to have a field down underneath. If you shoot down a ship, what have you got? The tank explodes, the *dinero* is destroyed, isn't it? So you've got to force them down so you can get at it. Now I can get around that."

"Continue," Von Sternberg said. There was a gleam of half amusement, half admiring interest in his eyes. He was still playing the god-like chieftain, but he was slightly more human.

"Well, I'm a stunt man," Groody told him. "You know, climb around on wings, change from ship to ship, and all that. I'll prove that to you any time you like, too. I've even been in the movies doing it. Here's what you do. Send out two ships on one of those jobs, or three if it's necessary, and get 'em anyway. It won't be a month, from what I hear, before every possible field will be guarded and you won't have a chance. The oil companies are set to stop your little depredation if it costs them a million bucks.

"Send out two or three ships, get the payroll ship dead to rights anywhere over the monte so that no one will know where or how you strike. One ship keeps its guns on the payroll ship and I'm in the other one with a pilot. We've got a ladder, or we can use any one of several other methods. Fly up close to it, I'll transfer, get the dough, change back, and that's that. I'm telling you, Count, you won't be able to operate forcing ships down the way you have been very much longer. They've got ships coming, and they've got a bird named Duke Daly that I'm pretty sure is going to work for them, and probably a bunch of other flyers coming in, and they're going after you right. If you must keep up the payroll stuff, that's the way to do it, but with the power and influence you've got, I'd lay off the oil companies and do something big, or if I didn't lay off them, get 'em quick and big and move on."

He stopped talking and was aware that James's eyes were resting on him with more interest. Von Sternberg suddenly seemed suddenly to be afire. The remarkable personality of that blond giant fairly crackled forth, and seemed to be like an invisible current vivifying the very atmosphere.

"How long have you been in Mexico?" Von Sternberg asked him.

Groody thought swiftly, "God, I'd give a year of my life to know whether he's playing with me or not!" And then, "Well," he said aloud, stalling for time, "That's another question that I don't know that I'd care to answer, Count. I know the spot I'm in. You can bump me off here and now—"

"I'm not a murderer!"

"If I thought you were, I wouldn't be here," Groody told him. "Nevertheless, I—"

TWO PISTOL SHOTS stopped his words as though a hand had been clapped over his mouth. Von Sternberg seemed to freeze behind his desk. A second later two more close together, and then, after a long interval during which the silence was unbroken, a final two crackled crisply through the air.

"Enough!" Von Sternberg said tersely. He pressed a button on his desk. "James, you and the Kid will take the air immediately. Hurry! But wait—"

He picked up the combination ear and mouthpiece on his desk.

"Manuel," he said into it. "Yes." He put the receiver to his ear and as he listened his lips parted in that wolfish grin and his eyes seemed to become colder and brighter.

"It is he," he snapped as he put the telephone back. "We shall see."

Taut as Groody had been, this quick interruption seemed to release springs in his body.

"What is it, Chief?" he said quickly as James turned to go. "Why the going into the air? Here's your chance to try me out."

That somewhat wolfish smile was playing over the count's face as he stood huge and commanding behind his desk.

"One whom I have been expecting is on his way by airplane," he said slowly. "His mission I do not know, or even that it is he. So you wish to be tried out, do you? Gott!"

The oath was like a pistol shot. Von Sternberg sort of crouched to listen. Very plainly there came to Groody's ears the drone of an airplane.

"James!" roared Von Sternberg, and his voice fairly shook the building. He was like some animal at bay and his face was now a bleak setting for eyes that blazed like a beast's. Every muscle in his huge body seemed tense as he threw himself around the desk and bounded to the door. "Manuel was asleep!" he roared. "He is here!"

Groody, his eyes dancing with a light that was like sun shining on ice, followed the big German out of the building. The Mexicans were searching the sky and talking excitedly, and the young German in the outside office followed them. James had stopped at the foot of the steps. The sun had set and the mountains cast shadows which submerged the camp.

Groody's ship was still on the line, but James's had been taken in, although there was no activity around the mouth of the cave which was evidently the shelter for the Von Sternberg airplanes.

Suddenly a ship hurtled into view across the north hills. It was so low that its undercarriage seemed to scrape the chaparral and as it came in sight it dipped down low.

Groody stood there as though paralyzed as he watched it. If that wasn't the ship which Penoch O'Reilly had flown across the McMullen airdrome in, it was its twin. He was literally paralyzed as he watched the plane swoop low down over the field. If it wasn't Penoch O'Reilly, who could it be? He could scarcely think for a second, and then it seemed as though he thought of a thousand things at once. Could he get to his ship and escape? Penoch was going to land, if it was he, though perhaps Von Sternberg had more than one of that type of a ship. Penoch's might not have been Von Sternberg's at all.

NO, O'REILLY WAS not going to land right then, at least. The motor of the monoplane full on, it came down to within three feet of the field. Von Sternberg was quiet now and everyone seemed to be holding their breath. The little settlement in the field was dotted with statue-like figures watching what was to happen next.

Suddenly the monoplane shot upward in a steep chandelle and something fell to the ground. As the ship started circling the airdrome, going ever higher, Groody saw a man run out on the field and pick up the object. Von Sternberg, without a word, threw himself on one of the horses, and Groody without conscious thought, leaped for the second one. The next instant he was tearing like mad down the street, following the outlaw chief.

Von Sternberg beat him by fifty yards. He dragged his

horse to a halt and flung himself off beside the man and read the note in one glance. Suddenly he seemed to have become very calm. His huge white teeth showed across his square face as his eyes rested on Groody with a peculiar gleam in their depths. Then they shifted to the plane circling above them. It was now at least a thousand feet high.

"Do you know of a Lieutenant O'Reilly," he asked slowly, his eyes meeting Groody's as though to look through him, "an American flyer, a Border Patrolman?"

"If I have met him, I've forgotten," Groody found himself saying. His brain was numb and for the moment he could not comprehend even a part of the significance of what was happening.

"How he comes here, or why, I do not know," Von Sternberg said.

Half a dozen men were grouped behind him at a respectful distance and Groody saw the Cactus Kid walk unhurriedly across the field.

"He and I have many things to settle. Read the note."

Groody, fighting for control of his chaotic thoughts, took the scrawled note and read it. It ran:

> *Von Sternberg: I dare you to come up and fight it out. We meet at five thousand feet and I'll wait for you, but if more than one ship takes off, I'll knock off every God damned one of you. Show some guts, you buzzard!—O'Reilly.*

For a moment there was silence as Groody's narrow eyes met the blazing ones of the outlaw.

"It is too important," Von Sternberg said, "that I not be

hurt for me to go up. You may not know it, but I was an ace in the War, and I am not a coward. You wish to make a place for yourself. You will go up in my place. I warn you he is a great flyer. You claim to be so good a pilot. Go up and get him, Mr. Dooly, and if you are a great pilot, you may, perhaps, get him alive. Should you do the first, you will have made yourself a place. Should you do the second, by accident or design, you shall be high in my organization."

For a moment Groody did not speak. Penoch was on the level!

"You hesitate," Von Sternberg said, his resonant voice booming forth more loudly. "Why do you not leap at this opportunity to prove yourself?"

Groody's body seemed to be a shell for a sort of fire within him which was reflected in his eyes and seemed to leap from every inch of his body. Now Von Sternberg was playing with him, but was there more to it than it seemed on the surface? Groody deliberately took out a cigar.

"Hell, there's no hurry. He'll wait," he said incisively. "Bringing him down is simple enough. I was just taking time out to figure how I could get him alive."

In the tense silence which ensued, during which Groody was conscious of the fact that there were dozens of eyes trained upon him, he suddenly regained complete control of himself. His mind was working like lightning, and it seemed as though every potentiality in the situation was as clear as crystal to him. Many apparently incongruous phases of the situation came into his mind unbidden, and he seemed able to scrutinize them calmly and appraise them for what they were worth.

Daly's words back in Tampico, hinting at mysterious

possibilities far transcending in importance mere payroll robberies, clicked into connection with the unusual effect his casual words suggesting such possibilities had had on both the Cactus Kid and Von Sternberg.

HE FORCED HIMSELF to forget for the moment what might lay ahead of him in the air and to blot out temporarily the thousand and one puzzling problems connected with O'Reilly's presence in that plane droning above them.

"Listen, chief," he said finally. "Come here a minute. I've got something private to say to you."

Von Sternberg came closer, while the ever-growing group behind him remained silent except for occasional quick, excited exclamations among them. It seemed as though the whole valley were waiting breathlessly for what might happen.

Groody's sloping lids were so low over his eyes that the pupils were barely discernible, and they never left Von Sternberg's eyes as he said, "Look here, Count Von Sternberg, you're asking me to go up in the air, fight a damned good flyer to death, risk my neck as well as my own ship in order to get a job I'm entitled to in the first place. Now just what is there in it for me? Just what do you mean? Suppose I prove myself a damned competent flyer, loyal to you, and get this bozo that you want to get, whoever he is. Where do I sit after I come down, if I do come down alive?"

"That," Von Sternberg said with a toothy grin, "is hard to say."

"I don't see why," Groody snapped. "Look here. You've got all the cards. Unless my ship has been gassed up, I haven't got enough gas to stay in the air three-quarters of an hour. I can't get away if I wanted to. Now I'll go up, and

I'll do what I can, providing I get what I want to out of it, and I'm taking your word of honor as a gentleman as all I need to go into the air."

"I promise you," Von Sternberg said, "a high place in my organization."

"And just how big is that organization, and what does that mean? Just a chance to knock off a few thousand bucks occasionally on a payroll robbery?"

Von Sternberg hesitated, studying the man before him with unwinking eyes.

"I tell you, Count, that's not enough. I'll take my chances right here on the ground, if I have to. My only reason for being here is the belief that there's something big up. My only reason for going into the air will be that I'm sure of it, and that I'm going to be somewhere in it. You're not taking any chances. Come clean."

Von Sternberg drew a long breath and his head came back as though what he was about to say required a pose in keeping with it.

"Suppose I should tell you that if you prove yourself worthy you can be high in the service of a government?"

There was a second of silence. Now Groody knew why the Mexicans had dressed as generals, and a thousand possibilities swarmed in his mind.

"O.K., Count. I'm on my way," he snapped. "Let's go!"

12

FIVE MINUTES LATER the Beed was taking off.

Groody glanced at the group of men in front of the cave's opening with a sort of savage sneer pulling at his lips. Then he looked upward as he took occasion to impress the men on the ground with a mighty zoom. Penoch was five thousand feet high now, circling warily. Groody drew a long breath and immediately forgot all things concerned with that camp down below as he faced the dilemma before him.

What in the name of God could he do after he got up there? He could arrange it so that Penoch would recognize him, but would the little flyer believe that he was a spy and not an actual member of Von Sternberg's gang? If he did succeed in convincing O'Reilly by signals that everything was all right, then what would he do? They could have a fake fight, and he, Groody, could pretend to be shot down—no, that would not do because it would leave O'Reilly the victor and the entire Von Sternberg organization would be in deadly fear of him, and it might spoil all plans.

WHEN HE HAD come there his idea had been in some way to kidnap the leader and bring him alive into Tampico. Now that was dismissed from his mind at least for the present. The first thing to do was to find out all the details of whatever gigantic conspiracy the abnormal German was heading.

His conversations with oil men had revealed much to him. In the last revolution literally hundreds of millions of dollars in oil had sprayed the countryside as the revolutionists deliberately destroyed well after well. Possibilities, domestic and international, were so vast that suddenly he felt as though the fate of those Americans in the oil district was on his shoulders, to say nothing of the friendly Mexican Government which it was the duty of an American government agent to consider.

Somehow the problem seemed to be a blank wall which had no opening in it. O'Reilly and Von Sternberg were deadly enemies, and yet—

In some manner and by some means he must arrange it, he decided, so that his own position would be unassailable and that O'Reilly would not be badly hurt.

As the Beed circled upward, Groody, his face suddenly drawn and pale below his tan, searched and searched for a way out. His mind cast around like a caged beast's trying to find a way of escape, and as the altimeter reached four thousand feet he was as far from a solution as he had been when he started from the ground. A thousand vague possibilities of different degrees of desperation occurred to him, and yet as he pointed the nose of his monoplane toward the higher ship there was only one thing clearly in his mind. That was that Penoch must know that he, and not Von Sternberg, was in that ship.

To that end, trusting Penoch not to attack until they met at an equal altitude, he climbed almost underneath O'Reilly's Falcon. How had O'Reilly discovered Von Sternberg's rendezvous, he wondered, and what had he been doing during the week which had elapsed since he had so mysteriously roared over the McMullen airdrome? Come to think of it, O'Reilly was absent without leave from the Army, and as this and other peculiar aspects of the situation came into his mind, his confidence in O'Reilly was subtly shaken. There might be many a nigger in the wood pile yet, he thought.

He was less than five hundred feet below the Falcon now, and as the climax loomed ahead of him, Groody's plight seemed too utterly hopeless to him, for at that moment there came a great revulsion of feeling. He forgot to be worried. It would do no good. The die was cast. He must get out of it as best he might.

He sort of straightened in his seat and it seemed that the reckless cast of his bold face increased. His lips widened in a sort of sardonic grimace as he prepared to let fate take its course.

The Falcon above him banked at right angles to its former course, as though to get away from the ship below. Now Groody did not follow it, but continued on his course, watching the Falcon unceasingly. Again the higher ship banked and Penoch's head came in sight, barely clearing the cowling on the side. Groody stared for a moment. Did Penoch have on a white helmet?

"By God, that looks like a bandage!" he thought, and a moment later he was sure of it.

COVERING THE LITTLE flyer's head completely, except for his face, was a dirty white bandage. Not only did it cover the top of his head but was wrapped down underneath his chin. There were big splotches on it which looked as though they might be blood.

The glasses he had had in the ship were still swinging from the side of the cowling, and now, with less than three hundred feet separating the two ships, he picked them up, raised his goggles and focused them on O'Reilly. Fairly leaping at him from the lenses was Penoch's face and Groody tensed as he saw it. O'Reilly had no goggles, and that white helmet was a blood-soaked bandage caked with dirt.

It was not this so much which caused his bewilderment to increase and his dread for the coming ordeal to deepen. The full faced little flyer he had known had changed until he was scarcely recognizable, had it not been for the little mustache, now bedraggled and drooping. O'Reilly's countenance was like a death's head. It was horribly emaciated, the cheeks sunken and the eyes deep in his head. He looked as though he was sick and starving.

Now O'Reilly seemed to be fascinated by the other ship. The two were flying side by side about two hundred feet apart and Groody perhaps a hundred feet lower than his prospective enemy. Groody himself had on no helmet, although he did have goggles on, and the wind was whipping his hair into a tangled mass.

He removed the glasses from his eyes and glanced below. They were a few hundred yards east of Von Sternberg's airdrome, and down on the ground at least fifty men were standing motionless, waiting for whatever might happen.

Groody, his goggles still raised, waved to O'Reilly to come closer. He signaled by every method he could think of to him, trying to make him understand that he wanted to delay the battle for a moment. Surely O'Reilly must have recognized him by now.

He opened the throttle wide and climbed more steeply toward the watchful little pilot. O'Reilly was leaning forward tensely, his eyes never leaving the other ship, as though alert for treachery but fascinated in spite of himself by what he saw.

Now Groody was within fifty feet of him. He pointed to himself, pointed down at the airdrome, signaled a dog fight with his hands and then a spin, endeavoring to make O'Reilly understand. Not a move came from the other ship.

He saw that O'Reilly, like himself, had a parachute on, and again he signaled first a dog fight and then jumps. Still no trace of recognition or comprehension from that statue-like little figure. He seemed utterly immobile, and again Groody raised the glasses.

O'Reilly's left wing tip and Groody's right were within thirty feet of each other, and they were flying side by side. Perhaps Von Sternberg might think that was funny, Groody reflected.

"Great God!"

It was more a prayer than an oath from Groody, as that face which seemed to be the reflection of a tortured soul bulked larger before the glasses. It was as though O'Reilly's eyes were within inches of Groody's own. O'Reilly's mouth was twisted into a snarl, and whether or not there was any sign of recognition in his gleaming eyes Groody could not tell, but this he was as sure of as the fact that he was five thousand feet above the ground at that moment. He was staring into the eyes of a man who was stark, raving mad.

HE DROPPED THE glasses and they flopped against the

side of the cowling. Then O'Reilly gestured with sublime contempt. One hand left the stick for a moment and he signaled to Groody to go west and himself east. Then abruptly he banked. He had not recognized Groody and the battle was on!

Groody banked to the left as Penoch had to the right. Never in his life had his spirit been depressed by such misery. There was a sort of bewildered pain in the rangy airman's eyes and at the moment it seemed as though there was nothing to do but to flunk it.

Heading upward, he watched the other ship. When the two were a thousand yards apart and at almost exactly the same altitude, Penoch threw his ship around in a vertical bank. Groody perforce did likewise. The next second, in the old tradition of specially arranged duels which had survived from the Western Front, the Beed and the Falcon were roaring at each other head on.

It was there that Groody snapped back to himself once more, and he settled down to fly for an objective which he did not quite know at the moment, but which occurred to him a few seconds later, and to fly as he had never flown before, and that meant plenty.

His throttle was all the way ahead and the radial motor's roar was like the unceasing roll of some giant drum. Using the speed he had generated, Groody made the first move just as red specks danced in front of Penoch's guns. Like a flash the Beed darted upward and no sooner had it gained a hundred feet than Groody had twisted it into a terrific vertical bank with the last remnant of speed.

The Falcon, which had zoomed likewise, shot upward almost underneath him, and Groody jammed the stick ahead. At that second the wily Penoch banked to the left and was shooting back underneath Groody and out of range.

What did that mean now, Groody was thinking grimly as he wing-turned his ship back on O'Reilly. He couldn't shoot. He did, though, time after time when he was sure that he could not conceivably hit O'Reilly.

The two ships were hurtling and diving and zooming through the air like two maddened animals. Burst after burst of machinegun fire came from O'Reilly's ship, but Groody, alert and strained, forestalled every move of the frantically flying Penoch.

The roar of two overwrought motors sounded like a thousand ships, and the universe was a combination of terrific blast and ear shattering sound as they fought their unceasing battle.

O'Reilly was a flyer, the haggard Groody decided with mounting desperation. Not one second was the Falcon still. Vertical banks, chandelles, terrific zooms, he never flew straight and level for an instant.

Bullet holes appeared in Groody's wings, and once as he was banking for a fake shot at the Falcon, one ripped through the flooring of the cockpit and missed his right foot by less than an inch.

A dozen times Groody himself had a fair shot at O'Reilly which he could not take. For the life of him he could not foresee the end of that terrific struggle. Only superflying had kept him from being shot down a dozen times by the madman who was his adversary.

THERE WILL ALWAYS be arguments as to who is the best flyer who ever stepped in a ship as long as flying lasts, but if ever Groody proved his right to the title which almost every flying student at Issoudun during the War had given him, it was that day. During his days as combat instructor, sending streams of advanced students up to the front whom he had trained, he became a legend, a lanky Nemesis with a cigar clamped in its mouth, who rode the tail of every student he had ever had without ever once being bested.

Thirteen Germans had fallen before his matchless flying when he had gone up to the front lines before he himself had been shot down by a formation of three, and all the skill that those years, plus the ones after the War had given him, he drew on now.

O'Reilly was flying with an utter desperation and increasing skill which forced the cold sweat from Groody's face, and time and time again caused him to give himself up for lost.

Groody was shooting steadily, but never when it could do any harm. He must end it some way, and quickly, or he would inevitably be killed or crippled by the little maniac who was flying as Groody had never seen anyone else fly before. No prospective collision caused him to falter for a second, and time after time O'Reilly took what would be disastrous chances if Groody had been fighting in earnest, in order to get in one deadly shot of his own.

The older man was forced literally to foresee the next move that O'Reilly would make, and hundreds of hours as a combat flyer came to his aid at times like that.

Just then O'Reilly came out of a wing turn ahead of him and with motor wide open dived down at him head on. Automatically, Groody banked swiftly to the left and dived. The next second he had twisted his ship around to the right, fairly underneath O'Reilly.

O'Reilly turned like a cat chasing its own tail and a blistering burst from a full nose dive would have surely been the last of Groody had he not jammed the stick all the way forward. The bullets got his tail surfaces instead of the cockpit.

Something seemed to snap within him as the other ship swooped down across his tail. It was now or never, he thought, as he pulled the stick all the way back. The Beed was traveling at nearly three hundred miles an hour, its laboring motor fairly shrieking as though in anguish. Upward and upward it climbed, and Groody's instinct for the air burst into full flower there.

He did not bring it over on its back immediately, but zoomed it almost straight up. He was so sensitive to flying speed that he could sense almost to the fraction of a mile exactly what flying speed he had. The Beed seemed to be going straight upward, standing on its tail, two hundred feet, three, four hundred, it cleaved upward through the air, and it was one hundred and fifty feet higher than an ordinary flyer would have allowed it to go before Groody's hand eased further back on the stick. Over it arched on its back, and then with the last remnant of flying speed it fairly tumbled right side up again as he used rudder and stick with all the sensitive skill at his command.

It came right side up just as O'Reilly, taken by surprise and now about three hundred feet below, zoomed his own ship and took a shot at the bottom of the Beed.

Once again, though, Groody was not to be taken by surprise. Almost as the Beed was coming level he had banked it to the right before he had ever noticed O'Reilly. Then to the left he went as O'Reilly dived to pick up speed and get out of danger.

IT WAS THERE that Groody, hunched down slightly in the cockpit, now, his head over the side, and his face like a leather mask, took his gamble. Downward went the Beed in a terrific dive, squarely at the ship below. Like a flash O'Reilly went into a vertical bank and at the same second the watchful Groody banked his own ship. The air speed meter needle was jammed up against the peg at two hundred and fifty miles an hour. Now he was flying on the same course as O'Reilly in that same terrific dive at him. Again O'Reilly banked, to the left this time, and again the Beed twisted on a dime and was following the lower ship relentlessly.

Groody could have jammed the stick all the way ahead and in a nose dive had a perfect shot at O'Reilly. Now O'Reilly, as though aware of his deadly plight, went into a continuous series of banks. Groody shoved the stick all the way ahead and then to right and left slightly, keeping a constant bead on O'Reilly. He was but a foot from him now, and he was forced to cover his nose with his hand in order to breathe if he was to look over the side. His goggles would not stay over his eyes and in one gesture he threw them away. His lids were closed down so low that his eyes were barely discernible. His eyes were flooded with the water called forth by the terrific air blast, as he followed his pitiful foe.

It was there that O'Reilly cracked. He could not shake off his Nemesis above, he must have decided, and he must get higher. He took the chance that only a madman would have taken. His ship went into a straight dive for a moment, Groody following him and overhauling him with every foot.

Then O'Reilly started arching upward. Without a split second's delay Groody pulled back on the stick of the Beed. The speed was so terrific that he had to use most of his strength to do it, and the slender monoplane was quivering as though it could not hold together for another minute.

Squarely ahead of him the other ship shot upward. He could have knocked Penoch off like a crippled duck at that moment.

With all the judgment of speed and distance that the years had given him, Groody zoomed his ship slightly. Now it, too, was darting upward at a slight angle, and he did not go wrong by so much as an inch. O'Reilly's ship was almost squarely on its tail as the Beed, like some huge aerial projectile darted toward it.

Groody used his rudder ever so slightly, without banking so much as an inch. The Beed skidded slightly, veering on its course without losing its equilibrium.

Groody did not flinch. His lean face like a drawn mask, he saw the other ship zoom slightly to his left. It was starting on its back. He got one fleeting impression of Penoch's frantic face looking up at him as his ship started over on its back. The next instant the left wing of the Beed ripped through the right wing of Penoch's ship.

There was a crash which transcended the roar of the motors for a moment as metal clashed against metal and linen tore to shreds. At the last second he had cut the ignition, but O'Reilly had not. The Beed's nose was snapped around and the two motors clashed together as the Beed's crippled left wing tore loose from the other.

THEN THE BEED'S wing snapped completely off before Groody's dazed eyes. The propeller of O'Reilly's ship appeared so close that it seemed as though it would cut him in two. Then it shattered.

His head was flipped forward against the cowling but a sheltering arm took the bruise. The ships seemed to be tumbling over and over in the air.

Only half conscious he loosened his belt and fairly fell overboard as his hand reached subconsciously for the ripcord ring of his 'chute. He fell five hundred feet before he opened it and as he pulled it, the rush of the air seemed to clear his head. He looked about him fearfully and then his body seemed to slump. There was O'Reilly above him, his 'chute safely opened, and almost even with them and but fifty yards away, the two ships, barely a foot apart, were whistling downward to their doom.

As though some spiritual second wind had come to him, all the strain of the past few hours dropped away from Groody and he felt a sort of exultant strength go through him. What was ahead he knew not, but so far he had won.

He looked below. They were at least five miles from the airdrome and he could see tiny figures mounting horses over there and he could sense some of the wild excitement which must be galvanizing those men. He had got Penoch and he had got him alive, but what would the future be when Penoch had been willing to fight him to the death?

13

IT SEEMED, HOWEVER, for the moment that the future could take care of itself, and dropping down through the quiet air was a moment's relaxation. Groody, his body swinging in ever-lessening arcs, let every muscle relax for a moment as he reveled in the peace which had followed that madhouse of roaring motors and spitting guns and screeching wires. Then as his ship hit the ground and exploded with a roar, he gathered himself together.

O'Reilly was coming down four hundred feet above him. He looked up at the little pilot and just as he looked he saw O'Reilly, a gun in his hand, taking a shot at him. For a moment Groody stared unbelievingly. He was too far away for any marksmanship with a six-shooter, but Lieutenant Percival Enoch O'Reilly was trying even then to shoot him down.

What was portended Groody did not allow himself to consider for a moment. His long arms went up to the shroud lines and in a trice he had gathered an armful of them and was pulling the size of his 'chute down. Handful by handful he pulled them in until he was dropping dizzily through the air. He must get to the ground before O'Reilly and cut him off.

"Thank God I've got a gun of my own," he thought.

Any doubt that he may have had of the fact that O'Reilly

had been turned into a species of maniac had left him, and suddenly the exultation which he had felt over his temporary victory died and once again he was walking a tight rope over disaster.

EIGHT HUNDRED FEET from the ground he released his 'chute once more and his speed gradually slowed to normal. The chaparral was thin and scraggly on the slope of the mountain below him, but nevertheless the landing presented difficulties. O'Reilly was about two hundred feet north of him so he would not have far to go after he had landed in order to receive him properly.

Groody's eyes sought the ground and picked up a tiny open space barely ten feet square in the midst of the gnarled mesquite. He was almost directly over it now and a hundred feet higher.

He dragged in the left corner of his 'chute and slipped it to ease his forward speed. He waited until the last minute and was dropping at least twice the normal rate of fifteen feet a second, when he released it just in time. He broke his rate of fall and with every muscle relaxed and his hand on the shroud lines he lifted himself as he struck. Pains shot through his legs and the bottom of his feet seemed numb, but he forgot that as he released his 'chute and ran to the spot where Penoch would land.

He jerked out his gun as he bounded through the undergrowth, and took four or five wild shots at the approaching pilot in order to warn him. Cactus ripped at his clothes and face as he made practically a bee line for the spot which would be directly underneath O'Reilly. He got there when O'Reilly was still two hundred feet high.

Again the little flyer shot at him. Groody dodged underneath a tree and shot back three times.

"Throw away your gun, or I'll get you sure as hell!" he shouted. "This is Groody, Penoch. Don't you know me. Listen, I'm not really with Von Sternberg. I'm here to get him. Be yourself—"

His answer was another shot.

Now O'Reilly was so close that his face was distinct. Twisted in an animal-like snarl, his sunken eyes glowing with a sort of unholy light, there was not a trace of sanity about him.

A few seconds later Groody saw him hit the top of a tree almost above where Groody himself was standing. O'Reilly had made no effort to Control his 'chute and his body hit the branches and bounced from one to the other with sickening thuds. The little flyer went limp. His body fell from the last limb but the 'chute caught in the top of the tree holding him suspended from the ground. He hung there, the gun still clutched in his hand, his head sagging limply from his shoulders, totally unconscious.

There were hot tears in Groody's eyes which had not known such a state of affairs for many years as he ran forward and tenderly released the pitiful little flyer. That bandage was splotched with clotted blood and his clothes were tattered and filthy. His heart was beating and a quick but thorough feeling with Groody running his hand over the limp little body, lifting the legs and arms carefully, showed that by some miracle no bones were broken.

HE SAT DOWN beside O'Reilly and relaxed for a moment. He had better wait for the horsemen. Then a thought came to him. He went over to where O'Reilly's parachute hung from a tree and arranged it so that it would billow upward, anchored to a high limb as a guide to the oncoming riders.

"God, I wonder what has happened in the last few days to make O'Reilly like this," he thought. "I don't believe he's eaten or slept for days. Maybe the last few months and this devilish Von Sternberg just naturally drove him cuckoo."

Then his thoughts veered in another direction. What would Von Sternberg do with his enemy now that he had him in his power? From all that Slim and the others had said, and from what he himself knew of the German, O'Reilly's physical safety was assured.

"Old Von won't stand him against any wall and shoot him," Groody thought. "God, if I could only talk sense to Penoch! They'll keep him a prisoner, of course. Have to, until we can get him out."

That brought up another swarm of potentialities. Groody would be forced to play out his string and if any one of the several more or less remote possibilities which were in his mind came to an actuality, the fact that O'Reilly was in the hands of his enemies would be a stumbling block. What if they said that O'Reilly's life was forfeit when the climax came, if any measures were used against them?

For a moment the tortured Groody felt that he had betrayed one of the Border gang, and yet what else could he have done? He had risked as much as O'Reilly and the stakes in this game transcended the immediate welfare of any individual.

For months and years the indomitable little flyer before him had fought his bitter battle with the Count, and—

"Maybe it'll be all for the best all around," Groody thought.

He looked down at O'Reilly's grimy face. There were new lines there and even in unconsciousness it seemed like a sort of horrible, emaciated mask. The cesspools of hatred and worry within him had made their mark and yet in that almost doll-like figure there was something more deeply pitiful than anything Groody had even seen. The mental, spiritual and physical wreck of the cocky little sparrow of a man lay before him.

From far away there came pistol shots and they recalled Groody to himself. His own gun spoke in answer and as the crackle of thickets and the voices of men became obvious he forced himself to forget Penoch and to lay his plans for the immediate future.

Tom was in Mexico City and receiving the secret cooperation of various government officials, and Daly would be at Querrara. He must get the news to them somehow and the immediate issue was how he could turn what had happened to the very best advantage. There were several possible methods of procedure, but as the Cactus Kid led his men into view, Groody had not decided on any one of them. He must let each moment take care of itself, he decided, and no definite plan made now would have much chance of success. There was one great objective he had in view and by some manner of means he must attain it.

THE CACTUS KID, riding like a centaur, came galloping toward him at full speed. His body swayed as gracefully as a reed as he dodged overhanging branches without slackening speed or altering his course. Behind him Wildcat Williams rode equally well and two Mexicans, each leading a riderless horse, kept the pace without trouble.

Groody stood up to meet them. The Cactus Kid, ten

yards in the lead, hauled up his horse with theatrical suddenness and flung himself off in one motion. It was almost dark but his grin flashed out at Groody and seemed to light up the shadows in some curious way.

"Was that an accident, or was it on purpose?" came that creamy drawl, and those eyes gleamed curiously at Groody as though illuminated by some inner glow.

"The chief wanted him alive, didn't he?" Groody stated, and deliberately took out his last cigar. "Well, he's got him."

The others came cantering up. The Mexicans gazed at Groody with a look of mingled wonder and respect and even the icy Wildcat Williams's sinister face held a thin-lipped smile.

"Well, Dooly, that was as pretty a fight as I ever saw," the Cactus Kid told him. "Congratulations!"

"Where in hell did you learn to fly like that?" Williams inquired and there was a gleam of acrid geniality in his eyes.

"Flyers yourselves?" Groody inquired.

They nodded.

"Well, then you know that it probably wasn't my first flight," Groody told them. "Now, listen, this little fellow's badly hurt. Fell into a tree. See that bandage and everything? We've got to make a litter and carry him between two horses."

They pieced together a makeshift litter with shirts and saddle blankets and Williams and Groody carried the still unconscious O'Reilly between them. As they made their slow way back to the airdrome Groody casually probed the feelings of his companions. By the time they had reached the settlement and were riding up the street before dozens of eyes, he was sure of one thing. Between the fake holdups and that battle in the air, he had won his spurs. Without conceit he felt more than that. His manner of arrival, his pose, and what he called the lucky breaks which had come to him, had won more than respect. In fact it seemed to him that there was a chance that he was looked on with only less bewilderment and puzzled admiration than the chief himself.

Which was no more than the exact truth. Not a man in camp, including Von Sternberg, but wondered who and what the lanky stranger might be.

THERE WERE TWO things, however, that they were sure of. One was that he was a remarkably fine addition to their number and the second one was that he was a man, who, for his prospects with the chief, and in his own right, it would be well to take at his face value, and not to fool with.

Groody roused himself from the trance he had been in during most of the ride and asked, "Is there anything that passes for a doctor around here? This kid ought to be taken care of somehow."

"Wolf studied medicine a while. He'll take care of him," the Cactus Kid told him. "We're supposed to go right to the chief."

The Mexicans left them and Groody, Williams and the Southerner rode up to the porch of headquarters. The two Mexicans who had been there before, augmented by General Lopez, were there, and as the cavalcade arrived they trooped down the steps and looked fixedly at the motionless body of O'Reilly. They exchanged more or less humorous remarks in Spanish, apparently, and while they did not speak to Groody, he could see that they were inspecting him with interest. They exchanged words which patently referred to him, and it was as though they were elated somehow at what had happened.

Groody himself climbed nonchalantly off his horse and said, "This boy's got to have a bed, and I don't mean maybe."

"He'll be put in headquarters, I'm pretty sure," Williams told him. "Let's carry him in."

Groody picked the little flyer up effortlessly and carried him up the steps himself. The German at the desk was coming forward as they entered, Groody leading the way.

"Where can I find a cot or something to put him on?" he said.

"The chief wants to see him first."

"The hell he does!" snapped Groody. "I'm telling you he needs a cot and I'm not going to haul him around any more. Where's this Wolf that's supposed to know something about doctoring?"

"I'm Wolf," the German said, apparently without resentment at Groody's harsh words. "Just a moment."

He went toward the door, but at that moment it was filled with Von Sternberg's huge figure.

"Ah, mein brusche!" he said, coming forward with a curious cat-like step. "You did well. He is not dead?"

"No," Groody told him, "but he's out like a light. He's been hurt before. Look at that bandage."

"Bring him in here," Von Sternberg said, leading the way into his office.

The outlaw was obviously greatly pleased with the situation. His eyes glowed and his toothy smile held more real enjoyment than it customarily did. It was as though he was mentally rubbing his hands in satisfaction.

"Thinks everything is breaking for him," thought Groody, "and he's congratulating himself on what a smart guy he is."

He laid Penoch on the big couch, and for a second the little group of men stood around him. It was almost entirely dark outside now, and the electric lights were on.

VON STERNBERG STOOD there for a moment, his eyes fairly devouring O'Reilly's wasted body. Groody, studying him, could not tell for the life of him what was in the German's mind. It almost seemed that Von Sternberg did not know himself what he was going to do.

"Well, it's a cinch he was bluffing back there in Tampico when he pretended that he got any information from Penoch," Groody thought for the dozenth time. "I'd give my little finger to know whether whatever's happened to Penoch between Laredo and McMullen was due to Von Sternberg."

"It strikes me," he said aloud, "as though this boy ought to be taken care of. I don't think any bones are broken, but I'm not sure. That bandage don't look so hot, either, and it's dirty as hell. I think, Wolf—"

As though Von Sternberg's steady gaze had stung him into life, O'Reilly moved slightly. Then his eyes popped open. For a minute they burned up at the huge outlaw. They were sunk so deeply in his head that it almost seemed as though they were looking through a mask, and the light of madness was still in them.

"So there you are, you jackal!" raved the little flyer suddenly, and his body came up like an opened jackknife.

Moving with the swiftness of a snake he swung his legs off the bed and started to hurl himself on his Nemesis.

Von Sternberg's arm shot out to stop him but Groody was ahead of him. He pinioned the little flyer's shoulders and stared down into that snarling, animal-like face. Steady, terrible curses came from those twisted lips, as O'Reilly's eyes blazed up at the square-faced Von Sternberg.

"There, there, boy. Take it easy," Groody told him, and his heart was pounding as though it would shake itself loose from his body. If O'Reilly recognized him, the whole works would be shot that moment—

But the little maniac did not. There was sheer delirium in his shouted curses and nothing but madness in those starry eyes. He did not know Groody from Adam, that was sure.

"He's nuts, chief," Groody said to Von Sternberg. "I tell you something had better be done for him, and quick."

He put his hand over Penoch's face and the Cactus Kid, those oriental eyes gleaming strangely, held his feet.

"Can he be taken care of here?" asked Groody. "It looks as though in your business, you'd have to have somebody that knew something."

"Johann can," Von Sternberg nodded. He was still looking down at Penoch with that unreadable gaze. There was something of wolfish satisfaction in his face, however.

"Well, no bird ever had his enemy in a worse spot than he's got O'Reilly right now," Groody thought.

"Johann," Von Sternberg said suddenly, "You and Cactus and Wildcat will take him over to Hut No. 2. You will see that he is cared for and do what you can for him."

"He's got a high fever," Wolf said. "I shall quiet him. He will be all right."

GROODY REMEMBERED FOR the first time that the man whom he had not seen, but who had been with Von Sternberg was Johann Wolf. Evidently the little German was another of Von Sternberg's right hand men.

As though the sudden effort had taken the last of his strength, O'Reilly seemed to slump and his tortured eyes closed wearily. He made no resistance as the three men carried him out.

Groody, his head whirling with the possibilities in the situation, had no more definite idea of what his next move would be, than he did of what was going on in China at the moment.

"Well *mein bursche,* sit down," Von Sternberg said suddenly. "You will be hungry. Yes?"

"I could eat the shirt off a statue," Groody informed him.

"Just a moment," Von Sternberg nodded, and pushed a button on his desk.

"We shall have sandwiches and beer here," Von Sternberg informed him. "Mr. Dooly, you are an excellent flyer. That was not your first combat."

"I'll say not."

Von Sternberg tilted back in his chair and there was a subtle difference in his attitude. He was still the superman, but it was as though he condescended to permit Groody more familiarity than before.

"You were not shooting to kill up there," Von Sternberg went on, his narrow, straight eyes playing over Groody with a sort of blinding light in them.

"Hell, no. You wanted him alive, didn't you, and I saw he had on a parachute. What have you got against him, anyway, Chief?"

Groody took special care to call Von Sternberg "chief,"

as though he took it for granted that he was a member of the band now.

"That is a long story," Von Sternberg told him, his lips parting. "Some years ago and occasionally since he took it upon himself to interfere with me and my plans."

"Which is unhealthy for anybody, eh?" Groody chimed in as the door opened and a young Mexican entered.

VON STERNBERG ORDERED sandwiches and beer and the young Mexican disappeared, his eyes darting a look at Groody as he left. It was very apparent that one ex-Lieutenant George Groody was temporarily the center of interest in the camp.

"Now, listen, chief," Groody said suddenly, "it's time for a showdown, and I think I've got a right to have it. I'm not forcing you, you understand, but I've done my part, haven't I?"

"Well—"

"Now, I'm going to say a few things at the start," Groody informed him. Somehow things had suddenly clicked into place in his mind and he had decided to gamble quickly and heavily. "I take it that a man as smart as you are has made up his mind to a few things right now. One is that I can fly and the other is that I'm the kind of a man you can use. Going even further, coming in here with the kind of a ship I did and under the circumstances that I did would seem to prove that I've got resources of my own, wouldn't it?"

"Well—" Von Sternberg said again. He sat there like a lion, as though waiting for a smaller and weaker creature to come within reach of him.

"What I'm getting at is," Groody went on, "that I don't

need you to live, understand? I'll eat and sleep regularly and get my share on my own, if I have to. If I hadn't got in that trouble on the Coast—"

"Yes? What trouble?"

"Doesn't amount to a great deal," Groody told him casually. "There are a bunch of flyers out there in motion pictures who, when business gets slack, can always run a little something over the Border from Aguas Calientes, Tia Juana or Mexicali—you know what I mean, so I just came down here for my health and to pick up a little *dinero*. I heard about you. I know what I can do, and furthermore I've got a few friends of my own, understand. I'm no penniless cheap skate, running around knocking off people for a few bucks. If I operate I intend to operate big, and if you weren't the kind of a leader you are, with the reputation you've got, I wouldn't be here. And if I didn't think that there were bigger things afoot than you'd ever done before, I wouldn't have been interested. I'd rather operate my own. Now I'm getting right down to brass tacks. I've got some assets of my own you can use, and I've got connections you can use."

"Yes? For instance?"

"Never mind. I'm well and favorably known to a lot of people, especially flyers, and you couldn't make three-quarters of 'em believe that I held up that payroll ship this afternoon, for instance. Anything you may want to do, especially on the Border, I can help you out on in a lot of ways. I'm not tipping my full hand, but I'm asking this. In view of what's happened today, can you use my kind of a man and whatever I've got besides myself to throw in, and if you can, how?"

FOR A MOMENT there was silence. Then Von Sternberg leaned forward, crossing his arms on the desk and it seemed as though lightning fairly leaped out from his eyes.

"Are any of those friends of yours at Querrara?" he asked, and his bass voice seemed to reverberate from the walls.

Groody's long body, lounging easily in his chair, stiffened. His face did not change.

"I'm not tipping my hand, I tell you, yet" he said and never had it been such an effort to be calm. Von Sternberg must have him right where he wanted him, and all his work had been for nothing.

"You see I know more than you think," said Von Sternberg. "You will find it well, Mr. Dooly, not to play with me. Your name is Groody, is it not?"

Groody, fighting to retain his poise and self-control, was able to say, "Well, with radios, and all that, there's no reason why you shouldn't. What if my name is Groody? Everybody in your gang doesn't go by their right handle, do they?"

Von Sternberg grinned.

"Not exactly," he said. "You had your ship at Querrara, and Donovan and Downs knew that you were leaving."

"Well, what of it?"

Never in his entire lifetime had Groody felt himself in such a desperate predicament. Von Sternberg had been playing with him, and he had been a doddering fool through the whole thing.

"So it would seem that there was much to be said," Von Sternberg went on with relish. "Shall I say what I believe to be the truth?"

"Sure," Groody told him.

"You fly down from Hollywood to Mexico, as you say," Von Sternberg said slowly, and Groody's heart leaped within him.

Then Von Sternberg did not know everything.

"And because of past connections which I do not know—yet, you find out much. I do things so easily you say to yourself, 'I, too, can be a Von Sternberg.' You get the information about the payroll ship and you think there is much money in it. Is it not so?"

"We'll talk about that later," Groody told him.

It seemed that every atom in his body was tense and waiting and that there was no part of him which was not sensitive to whatever implication might lie in Von Sternberg's words.

"You had some scheme to get the money and still maintain your position. This was spoiled by the arrival of my ships. You had thought yourself above suspicion by your friends and the holdup would be laid to me. Not so? Accidents happen. Your loop was small. You see your opportunity and you come here."

Groody was hard put to it to keep from drawing a great sigh of relief. Von Sternberg in his desire to be all-knowing and impress him, had given away his hand. That he was allied with Daly and Service, Von Sternberg did not know. The German was not playing with him now. He was certain of that as he was that he was sitting there.

IN A SPLIT second thousand things seemed to go through his mind. That fake holdup had been effective, and even more, that battle over the camp would be conclusive evidence to anyone, now that he came to think of it. He had builded better than he knew.

"How you knew," Von Sternberg went on spaciously, "that I, too, have two Beed airplanes and that there was no way it could be known that you were not a member of my organization, I do not know, or did you know that?"

"No, chief, I didn't, for sure," Groody told him. "Boy, I'll say that you know your onions. You've figured it right out to a T. I did think I could pick up some coin without being suspected because any hijacking in the air would be laid to you anyway. Why, I was even considering getting a job, if I could, flying payrolls for the oil companies. You see, to them and to most people, any little slipping off the straight and narrow path I've done since I got out of the Army would be unbelievable. I've got a reputation, believe it or not."

"Your reputation was known to me in France," Von Sternberg said. "You were at Issoudun, were you not?"

Groody nodded. Somehow it didn't seem possible that he could get away with what he wanted to, and yet that battle over the camp and that hold-up evidently were doing the trick.

The Mexican entered with the sandwiches and a half dozen bottles of beer. When he had left, Von Sternberg did not offer to touch the food, nor to allow Groody to.

"You see, Mr. Groody, I know a little about you. I know of your being in South America, that you are a soldier of fortune. I can use you if you are loyal. You have passed the tests I gave you and I have no fears, for this reason."

"What reason?"

"Because you will not live one hour if you should prove the contrary," snapped Von Sternberg. "Not in Tampico, not in Querrara, not in the remotest reaches of Mexico."

For a moment Groody studied him. How in the name of God did he have all the information from Querrara? His very assumption of omnipotence was his weak point in the situation. That Groody, in some lucky fashion, through his pose as a member of the crew of the *Pride of Galveston*, had given Von Sternberg the slip at the start, the fact that he thought he knew everything, had turned into Groody's greatest asset.

"Count, I told you I was out for the coin. Just how can you use me? I admit everything, and I'm here."

"Furthermore," Von Sternberg went on, his voice more resonant than usual and louder, as though he was convincing himself as well as Groody, "I do not fear more than an individual traitor. I do not fear an army. There is no power in Mexico today that I fear. I will defend my stronghold here with success against the Federal Army. Should you, or any of my men, go back and tell where I was, everything about me, I still would live. So you see, even though I were not sure of you, that I would be taking no chances."

"You don't have to prove that to me," Groody told him. "You have been operating for years, and you haven't been doing it without knowing where you were. Good God, I come out here and see a perfect fortress. God knows how many ships you've got. I see Mexican generals sitting around your front porch, I see radios and electric lights and all the comforts of home way back here in the woods. And that, Count Von Sternberg, is why I want to be with you."

"If only you were not an American!"

VON STERNBERG GRINNED that animal-like grin when he said that, and in a flash there leaped into Groody's mind what Graves and the others had told him. That the count was a man of many complexes and prejudices was very obvious after one knew him. His almost insane desire to think of himself as all-powerful was in fact the greatest single evidence that there might be no limit to his future plans, or to the audacity of them, which might readily reach to the point of being foolhardy.

"I know you haven't any love for the States," grinned Groody. "I always wondered why a fellow like you amused himself trying to steal dirigibles which wouldn't get you anything."

Von Sternberg's grin was really boyish then.

"To prove them the fools they are—the body of a giant, the brains and background of a child of the slums."

"Mr. Groody," he said suddenly, and all traces of mirth were wiped from his square face, his jaw set, "I can assure you. In all my organization I have no one that can do what you have a chance of doing. You will fly one of my Beeds to wherever it was you were supposedly starting for from Querrara this afternoon. You will tell a tale of a forced landing in some remote place. Where were you going?"

"To Tampico," Groody lied.

"There you will endeavor to hire yourself out as one of the special men whom the oil companies are gathering in an attempt to destroy me. You will be my liaison man, giving me all the advance information you can pick up by methods I will tell you. Then, *mein bursche,* I may use you upon the Border, if you prove yourself worthy."

"That's the talk!" barked Groody. "And even if I can't get a job, and I think I can because I know Daly, who is down here—"

"You know him?"

"Sure I do," grinned Groody.

THE DESPERATE GAMBLE in mentioning Daly he thought the best strategy, and he was right. His apparent frankness seemed to impress Von Sternberg. Surely that would be one thing that he would try to hide if he were a spy.

"Ah! That is good!" nodded Von Sternberg.

"And even if I can't catch on there, I can buzz around and maybe pick up some stuff that your other men can't. By the way, I'd better know who your men are."

"Ah, but no."

"Why not?"

"They will know you, but you will not know them," Von Sternberg told him, "and if but once you should be persuaded to go wrong, punishment will be swift and sure."

"I see," Groody said slowly. "Still not completely satisfied, eh, chief?"

"Satisfied, yes, but I take no chances. There is no one man that I trust. Whether I should go so far with you in ordinary circumstances, I do not know. I have no one to use. James, yes, but too well known. The Cactus Kid, Williams, those others—bah! They are crazy youngsters unfit for responsibility for big things. The Mexicans, they are children. The men I could trust, like Johann and the others, they are known as I am known. Their usefulness as spies is over. The others in the length and breadth of the oil fields, they are competent for only one little job at a time to give information. You, although an American, I may use much in the future."

"Regarding that future, now that we're all set, chief," Groody said, eyeing the sandwiches hungrily, "I'd like to go into it a little bit. Before I went in the air you said a few things. What are you planning to do, be President of Mexico, or something?"

"No. We shall see in due time," Von Sternberg told him. "We shall eat, no?"

14

APPARENTLY, VON STERNBERG'S temporary burst of frankness, which had been induced by the climax of the afternoon, was over. He withdrew into his shell as he and Groody tackled the sandwiches and the beer in his private office. The Mexican was rung for again and additional beer was procured. Groody was a valiant imbiber and was possessed of two hollow legs. As the evening wore on and the beer mellowed Count Von Sternberg, he talked more and more of the past. It was as though he sensed something in the rangy American flyer which made Groody more of an equal than any of the other men he had about him, and it pleased him to feed his ego by bragging.

Hour after hour passed, and bottle after bottle died the death of a dog as Groody prodded his host on with interested questions. The war was fought over, then more immediate things gone into, and gradually bit by bit the grandiose plans of the huge outlaw were hinted at. There was nothing very definite, but by the time Groody had stumbled off to bed he knew much more than he had known before. That there were dozens and dozens of *jefes* throughout Mexico who had been biding their time before overthrowing the governmental regime, Von Sternberg had proved to him. That throughout the length and breadth of the oil fields, particularly, the Mexicans resented what they considered the exploiting of their country by the Americans, a state of feeling which Von Sternberg proved to be a sort of abscess on the body of Mexico which would soon come to a head.

Over the years when he, to satisfy himself, had made it his business to harry the Americans, he had built up more than admiration in the breasts of thousands of humble peons. He had the Secret cooperation of local chieftains far and wide. Many and many a sizable Mexican town was a perfectly safe headquarters for Von Sternberg and his men, and Groody went to sleep that night with the firm conviction that the big outlaw was planning to be, and was perhaps able to be, the greatest single factor in some upheaval which might shake Mexico to its depths. In his own way he was already a successful rebel against constituted authority, and if those generals on the porch, and if Von Sternberg's grandiose words meant anything, it meant that he was adding to his power with every passing day.

For a few minutes, worn out as he was, real slumber would not come to Groody. Penoch O'Reilly, the thousand unseen enemies who would be surrounding him on all sides, even in Querrara, how he was to survive until his information was complete enough to do something definite, all these considerations swarmed through his mind in a sort of devil's dance.

He believed Von Sternberg when he said that he did not fear the exposure of his remarkable headquarters. His power was too widespread and his resources too vast for that. The death or capture of the outlaw would not necessarily stop what was afoot, either. Broad hints about how the United States was to be used, which Groody could not get head nor tail of, was an additional factor.

He felt as though he were up against a blank wall, and running around like a rat trying to find a way out.

"Well," he told himself drowsily, "there's so much to think about, there's no sense in thinking at all. Tomorrow, maybe—"

And he drifted off into dreamless deep.

HE HAD BREAKFAST the next morning in one of the huts which was used as a mess. He was somewhat late, but Williams and the Cactus Kid were still dallying over their coffee. As he entered the hut to which he had been directed by Wolf, the Cactus Kid gazed at him with an unreadable look in those peculiar eyes.

"Got drunk with the chief last night, did you?" he drawled.

"I wouldn't exactly say that," Groody stated as he sat down at the board table.

"You certainly spent plenty of time in there," Williams said.

Both men were looking at him with a subtly changed attitude, which Groody sensed immediately.

"Well, what did he do?" the tall Southerner said with a careful attempt at being casual. "Hire you as the head man, or something?"

"Oh, at least that, I'll bet," Williams chimed in.

"No, not exactly," Groody told them as he thought, "I'm a son-of-a-gun if they're not sort of sore."

"Didn't he give you any steers?" The Cactus Kid asked him.

"No, not particularly," Groody replied as a Chinese brought him some sort of a cereal. "I'm leaving this morning in one of his Beeds to see what I can do on the outside."

"You're leaving!" little Wiliams said in utter amazement.

"Sure. I've got plenty to attend to for the chief around

Tampico and other spots." The two outlaws looked at each other wordlessly. Then the Cactus Kid got to his feet.

"Well, Wildcat," he said in that creamy drawl, but somehow it was not so attractive then, "it looks as though somebody was moving to the head of the class, don't it? Remember your place, now, Wildcat, and walk slow and easy."

It was utterly apparent that the two outlaws had become jealous of Groody's position. They left the hut as Groody was mulling over the possible results of their attitude. Evidently it was not Von Sternberg's habit to fraternize with his subordinates as he had with Groody.

"That Cactus Kid fellow fancies himself quite a bit, too," Groody reflected. "The way he bosses everybody around, including Mexican generals, shows that he figures I'm moving in and that he won't be such a complete cock of the walk as he has been. Well, that'll have to take care of itself."

An hour later, after a few last words with Von Sternberg, he and his headache roared over the limitless monte in a Von Sternberg Beed.

There were ten ships of various types in that huge cave, and a veritable arsenal of machine guns and ammunition. The ship he was flying was a standard plane, as the one he had flown into the place was, and painted the same bluish gray color.

DURING THE TWO hours and a half it took him to get to Tampico he had plenty of time for thought and, somehow, as he gazed over the vast reaches of Mexico, he was conscious of a curious feeling of fear. It seemed like a monster brooding under those coverings of chaparral in the luxuriant jungle, and as he thought of all the hidden forces at work, he felt as though he were some helpless insect entangled in a huge web.

There were so many sides to his position that it seemed as though there was no way for him to turn without facing a catastrophe. Penoch O'Reilly back there, sick and out of his head, the whole nation below him thick with spies, he felt as though there was nothing he could do which could result in success by anything but a lucky chance.

Von Sternberg's superb self-confidence was more nerve-racking than outright suspicion would have been. The fact that he was setting Groody loose was proof positive that he did not think Groody, even if a traitor, could hurt him. That meant that his grandiloquent hints of far reaching power were not made of the stuff of dreams.

Gradually the chaparral merged into thick undergrowth and he was over the jungle. An hour later the town of Panuco came in sight and he was soon spiraling down over the flying field two miles west of Tampico as the air became hotter with every hundred feet he dropped. After he had landed it seemed as though he had plunged into a warm enervating bath.

An hour later, in the cool fastnessess of the Imperial Hotel bar room he was talking perfectly openly with Duke Daly. He felt that that was the best strategy that could be employed. No efforts to secrecy, he felt would be of any avail.

Daly, cool and calm and level voiced, had greeted him casually but as the tale was unfolded, his eyes glowed warmly and Groody could feel the spirit behind that good looking mask of a face.

"Now," Groody concluded, "the way I see it, there's just

one way to work. I've got to pull one more thing within the next day or two to wipe away all doubt in Von Sternberg's mind. We've got to work fast because God alone knows what'll come off when Penoch gets his wits back. Hell will be popping all over the place, if I'm any judge, unless I can get to him before anybody else does. By the way, I must wire McMullen about him. How in hell do you suppose he ever found Von Sternberg's spot? There isn't a landmark within fifty miles, unless you are in the know. They have little clearings cut here and there to guide the way, but an outsider wouldn't know it."

Daly shook his head. He was gazing absently at the wall, his hand playing with his untouched glass of beer.

"I don't know," he said. "Probably his delirium will be a sufficient excuse for his absence without leave from the Army, though."

SUDDENLY HIS EYES met Groody's, and it was as though a curtain had dropped over them to hide his thoughts.

"So there's a spy at Querrara," he said slowly, "and you've got to cement your position with the Count. I don't think that persuading the oil man to risk a few thousand more dollars would be effective enough. You can work in the open with me now. In fact, that will mean more than any attempted secrecy."

One of the bar attendants came up and started wiping down a nearby table. Daly jerked his head toward the man and Groody got the meaning he hinted. He might be a Von Sternberg spy. They talked casually until the man had left and then Groody said with a sardonic grin, "I feel as though there were about a thousand eyes and ears around me all the time. This lack of privacy is getting my goat."

Daly nodded unsmilingly.

"I think I have the proper scheme," he said slowly. "See what you think of it and if you like it, we'll wire Service in Mexico City what we're going to do. He and I have a code fixed up, by the way, so we don't need to be frightened, and it may affect his plans a little."

"Is he getting any dope down there?" Groody demanded.

"I don't know. He's going to have the cooperation of the embassy. He wants to uncover just how much, if any, influence Von Sternberg wields at the capital. It's a cinch he must have some down there, not officially, of course.

"Well, what have you got figured out?" Groody demanded.

The contained Daly told him quietly and with no more emotion discernible in him than there was in the table between them. Cool and blond, his face expressionless, he unfolded his plan while Groody's eyes grew narrower, and his cigar in his mouth went out because he forgot to draw on it.

As Daly finished silence fell for a moment, broken only by the whir of the electric fan in the deserted bar. Then Groody very deliberately flipped the dead ashes from his cigar. He thrust one hand across the table.

"Let's shake on that, Duke," he said quietly.

How and why the "Duke" had slipped out, he could scarcely have told himself.

"It's a go?" Daly asked quietly.

"Good! God, man," Groody exploded, "of course it's a go as far as I'm concerned! You're the one that will be taking the rap." Suddenly his eyes glowed more warmly and his mouth widened in that one-sided smile. "Maybe a little hell can be raised that way, at that, eh?"

"I think so, perhaps," Daly smiled and suddenly that warmth leaped into his eyes again. "We'll try it out, and listen, George, don't be too easy on me."

"I won't," Groody promised. "Let's get under way. The quicker, the sooner, eh?"

ALL DURING THE time they were on the way to the field and flying their two separate ships to Querrara, Groody was conscious of the fact that he had more hope than he had had before. It seemed as though a ray of light was penetrating the gloom of his position and suddenly life was a more enjoyable and satisfactory thing than it had been before.

"And there's no particular reason for it," he thought to himself, as the monte rolled away below him, "except that that devil Daly is going to help out, and that's a tribute, doggone him!"

And it was, for Groody, aside from Tom Service, was a born lone wolf who ordinarily asked no odds from anyone or anything.

At Querrara they waited at the field for a car to come and get them, having flown over the camp to signify their presence. The pipes in the boiling sun were as white as snow, covered with frost. The carbon dioxide gas congealed even in that boiling sun, as Daly explained.

"You're absolutely sure of Downs and Donovan?" Groody said for the tenth time as a tool pusher in charge of a Mexican came clattering down the rough road.

"Absolutely!" Daly said. "That is, suspicion of them would be as unthinkable as suspicion of you, for instance.

Furthermore, if either Donovan or Downs was a spy and Von Sternberg did get his information from either one of them, he would have known the whole reason for your being at his camp and you wouldn't be horsing around free the way you are, nor would you have been sent up to bring down O'Reilly, or anything else."

They climbed into the tool pusher and a few minutes later had collected Mr. Kid Donovan and Bib Jack Downs in the little shack next to the dehydrating plant which was Downs' office.

GROODY EXAMINED THE plant briefly. It was a mass of coiled copper pipes, complicated with boilers, vats, and other machinery which were a total mystery to him.

"Well, well, well!" the genial Downs said with a boyish grin on his full face. "Back safe and sound, huh? What happened, big boy?"

"Plenty," Groody told him. "To make a long story short Von Sternberg fell for that fake holdup and now I'm here as a spy of his."

"I'd like to hear all about it!" chuckled Downs, his dark eyes sparking.

"We're in a hurry. I'll tell you about it later," Groody informed him.

"Where's Dr. Gross?" Daly asked.

"Went to Tampico this morning and will be back late tonight," Downs said. "Why? Did you want to see him?"

"In a way, yes," Daly said evenly, "but I guess you'll do."

"What's on your mind?" barked Donovan, his bright little eyes searching the faces of the two airmen.

"We don't quite know," Groody said. "Listen, what kind

of a guy is this old doctor? He's the inventor of this dehydrating thing, isn't he?"

"This particular adaptation of it, yes," Downs said soberly. It was as though he sensed matters of import behind the words of the two flyers.

"Well, have you got something here that's going to make you a lot of money?" Daly asked.

"Can't tell yet," Downs told him. "I don't know what you boys are getting at, but I suppose it's something. The idea is this, there's a lot of oil comes out of the ground, especially around here, so mixed up with water that it's no damn good. In order to reclaim that oil, the globules of water around the particles of oil have to be cracked to release the oil. There's only one way to do that, and that's by heat. This oil down here, a lot of it, is so damned bad that the ordinary methods haven't worked. Dr. Gross got the idea of dehydrating the oil under pressure. That is, we move the oil through these pipes under pressure, consequently can use enough heat to do a good job, we think, without the evil effects of terrific heat acting on the oil."

"How did you get in touch with him?" Daly asked.

"I had some money and ran into him up in the Smackover Field," Downs informed him. "I put in all my dough to back him and then later on the International Oil Company that runs this station put in some dough to build this plant for Gross to experiment in."

"Well, how are you making out?" Groody asked him. "Don't think we're just idly curious, Downs. You'll see what we're getting at."

"Lousy," Downs said frankly. "He's lost us thousands of dollars. He thinks his scheme is so damned good that he's always insisting on trying to work this plant to more than its capacity. We've burned out pipes, had all the troubles in the world, simply because the old fool is trying to put a two-ton load on a one-ton truck. He's cuckoo. The son-of-a-gun came near killing me with an ax the other day. He's bugs, but I'm in so deep I can't cut loose from him now."

"Then he hasn't got any money of his own, or anything to speak of?" Daly slid in.

DOWNS SHOOK HIS head. "No, and he figures International, and I, and about everybody else in the world is trying to steal his invention from him and freeze him out."

"Oh-ho!" said Groody. "Daly, maybe your hunch wasn't so far wrong. Listen, gentlemen. You know what I found out when I got to Von Sternberg's headquarters?"

"I can think of several things," Donovan said. "Which one do you mean?"

"Just this," Groody said slowly. "There's a Von Sternberg man here at Querrara. Von Sternberg had plenty of dope about me. Everything, in fact, except that the holdup was faked. Someone here told him that my ship left from here and who I was. The question is who is that spy, and on account of Dr. Gross being German, and Daly hearing a lot of gossip about how he wasn't getting along with anyone, he naturally figured on him. Von Sternberg works a lot by radio. Ever seen any signs of Dr. Gross having one around?"

The two oil men looked at each other wordlessly.

"Listen," Donovan said suddenly, "if there is a spy in this camp it could hardly be anybody else but Gross, Jack. These laborers around here ain't got any idea of who Groody is. Can't have. Did you ever let drop anything to Gross, Jack?"

"By God, yes!" exclaimed Downs. "George was introduced around as Dooly to a few of the boys and I'd vouch for every one of 'em, and there wasn't anybody but you and me that knew who and what he was. The doc and I were getting on pretty well a few days back. He gave in on those new coils I wanted and I was feeling pretty friendly. I did spill the beans to him, and as for a radio, he's got a little shack back in the woods, a sort of a study, where he goes to be alone every once in a while. He's sort of cuckoo as I said. I wonder if there might be something there."

"We can soon find out," Donovan said. "Let's go, boys, while we've got the chance."

Half an hour later they were breaking down the door of a small wooden shack three-quarters of a mile from the camp in the middle of a small clearing. It was furnished with one easy chair, a couch and a desk, and a bookcase filled with many scientific books.

THEY WENT OVER it inch by inch. There was no sign of an antenna or anything of the sort and Groody had just about abandoned hope when an excited yawp from Downs caused him to come out of the small, utterly bare room which was in the rear of the larger one.

"How do you like *these* apples, gentlemen?" Downs crowed. "I was just trying this bookcase and look what happens."

The book shelves, about five feet wide and four tiers high swung outward like a door, and behind it there was a radio sending and receiving apparatus. It took but a few moments to trace the wires which ran under ground.

"Somewhere or other, maybe several miles from here, the son-of-a-gun has got the machinery to send and receive messages," Downs said.

"No need to track that down now," Groody snapped. "Duke, we might as well lose no time. My idea is, now that we've got the absolute dope, to work like this, if we can get the oil companies to do it. Think they'll risk a few thousand more?"

"Sure," Daly said, his voice vibrant, "now that we're right on the track. They'd be dumb-bells not to. I'll wire Service so that the government can be notified in Mexico City and also tell 'em to lay off until we get all the dope."

As though the finding of that radio set had touched some spark in him, Daly's cool exterior seemed to be warmed and vivified by the emotion within him. He seemed younger somehow, and utterly boyish in contradiction to that weariness and indifference which usually characterized his attitude.

"Von Sternberg just got to this old cuckoo who thinks he's so mistreated and bedeviled by everybody," Donovan said, astonishment and bewilderment fighting for priority in his face. "What do you know about the old coot!"

"I'll leave you fellows to put everything shipshape," Daly said spaciously. "I'll beat it back to Tampico. Let's give the doctor plenty of rope until we know what we're doing. Maybe we can use him. Don't tip your hand, either of you, whatever you do. Groody, you'll hear from me tonight."

Which Groody did shortly before Dr. Gross reached camp from Tampico. Groody barely saw him, a bent, whispy little figure with a scraggly gray beard and tremendously thick glasses over very bright little eyes. He looked as harmless as a child.

Results of Daly's trip to Tampico were many. One of them was that at nine o'clock next morning Daly's ship was on the ground in the same field that the Duke had landed on a few days previously. Groody was flying over it. Daly got out and walked slowly to the end of the field while Groody swooped down and poured a burst of machine gun bullets into the fuselage between seat and tail. A few bullet holes were added to the wings. After that Groody came down to land for a last confab with his ally.

AS HE LANDED and Daly came walking toward him, Groody saw with surprise that Daly's left hand was bleeding profusely. In the Duke's right hand was a roll of bandages and a bottle.

"Well, what the hell happened to you?" Groody said in amazement.

Daly grinned.

"Shot myself through the side of the hand—by accident," he said calmly.

Groody took a quick look at the flesh Wound. Then his eyes met Daly's.

"You son-of-a-gun," he said slowly. "You did it deliberately to make this whole thing more convincing!"

"Well, what of it?" said Daly his eyes dancing with that boyish light. "Stick some of this antiseptic on it and bind it up for me, will you?"

Groody did so, silently, and did not refer to the subject again but it scarcely left his mind for hours. The bandaging completed, they sat down in the shade of the wing of Groody's ship for a cigarette, as they talked things over.

"I guess that sets it," Groody finally said as he stood up. "The whole point is to force their hand and put 'em on the jump right now. Got everything set where and how we first met, and the whole works?"

Daly nodded.

"Let's go," he said quietly.

They took off for the long trek to Von Sternberg's headquarters, Daly flying in front in his bullet-riddled ship, and two hours later Groody was escorting his supposed captive up the street of the settlement to Von Sternberg's office. He had his gun out for theatrical effect and beside him walked James, Williams and the Cactus Kid.

James said nothing, but the Kid and Williams tried steadily to extract information which Groody refused to give them. At the foot of the steps the Cactus Kid gave up the job.

"Well, go on in and get patted on the head," he said finally, but as Groody and James and Daly walked up the steps to greet Wolf at the door, Groody thought he heard Wildcat Williams say: "It smells pretty fishy to me."

Groody glanced at Daly and Daly's eyelids flickered. He had heard it, too.

"It looks to me," Groody remarked to James, "as though there was a little jealousy among the troops."

James' bulging eyes glanced down toward the retreating figures of the two outlaws.

"Don't worry," he said mildly. "The chief will attend to them. He has before."

INSIDE THE DOOR Wolf's close-set eyes rested on Daly and he bowed meticulously, his heels fairly clicking in the gesture.

"We meet again," he said.

"So it seems," Daly said evenly.

"Tell the chief we're here," Groody told him. "By the way, how's O'Reilly?"

"Somewhat better," Wolf said as he started for the door, "but he just lays there and does not say a word and I do not think he yet knows all that has happened. His delirium should be over soon."

A moment later Groody and Daly walked into Von Sternberg's office. The big German's eyes were like searchlights in his head as he sat behind his desk.

"Why and how does this happen, Groody?" he asked slowly. "We do not want prisoners."

"I think you'll want this one, chief," Groody told him, "if we can knock the truth out of him. May we sit down?"

"Of course."

"O.K. I'm tired. Now listen."

Groody took time to light a cigarette in substitution for his exhausted supply of cigars and mentally gathered himself together for the greatest gamble of them all, so far.

15

VON STERNBERG SAT like a huge statue behind his desk. As though recollecting himself, he smiled his toothy smile at Daly.

"We meet more frequently than I had thought," he said, as though playing a part without having a great deal of interest in it. It was plain that his mind was on more important things. "It is good of you indeed to return my call."

Daly, cool and impassive, did not so much as smile.

"I didn't do it voluntarily," he said.

"Incidentally," Groody cut in, "I brought a few thousand bucks along with me to throw into the kitty, chief. Daly just happened to have it with him."

He tossed the package, which he took from his shirt, on the desk. Von Sternberg did not offer to touch it. He was looking at Groody as though that lose-jointed gentleman was a very curious and interesting person.

"I also figured," Groody went on, "that another ship wouldn't be unwelcome."

"But this money and that ship—they were not the reasons for the annoyance of a prisoner?" boomed Von Sternberg.

"Not a bit of it Chief, I found out plenty on this trip, but not all of it, and I figured that we might have the means of getting the whole truth out here in the woods. In the first place, I know that your man at Querrara is Dr. Gross, and furthermore, a lot of other people know it."

Von Sternberg seemed to freeze.

"Yes?" he asked swiftly and it was as though he had unobtrusively gathered himself together to strike.

"Exactly. By a lot of other people, I mean two or three people that count. Dr. Gross doesn't know that he's suspected himself, but everything from that hidden radio set of his in the shack to the fact that he communicates with you is known. They didn't let me in on all of it, I being more or less of a stranger, and not very well known even to Daly here, but I swear I figure that more is known by your enemies about what you are doing and intend to do than you have any idea, and if you're going to move, you'd better move fast before they unwind the whole snarl. Understand?"

VON STERNBERG SAT there quietly as though unable to believe his ears. His eyes stared into Groody's and suddenly they had become bleak and cold. It was obvious that behind that square face and those cool gray-green eyes his mind was working with lightning-like speed; so much so that he forgot to say anything.

"Now, Daly," Groody snapped, turning to him, "it's up to you to shoot the works. I'm not ordinarily bloodthirsty, but my neck's in this noose as well as the chief's, now, and it's a case of shoot the works. You've got to spill all you know, and if necessary I'll forget my bringing up and use some methods that wouldn't be very sweet, if the chief'll let me, to get it out of you."

"You don't say?" Daly said evenly. "Suppose I don't know anything?"

"The hell you don't!" Groody told him flatly.

Von Sternberg was like a referee, gazing at them both, and he seemed content to let Groody go on.

"We know that you're down here for the oil companies, but how many men you've got or what resources you've got, we're not sure of. That *you* practically run the works, and that you've got a lot of information collected and a lot of schemes afloat is just as plain as the nose on your face. You wouldn't be giving Dr. Gross all the rope you're giving him if you didn't have an idea that by so doing you could gain more complete knowledge of certain plans. We've got certain plans."

He got to his feet, his lips twisted into a mirthless grimace.

"Now, Mr. Daly," he said, lounging over toward the poised flyer, "you come clean, and do it fast."

Daly got to his feet slowly as though to meet the menace of the taller man who was towering over him.

"Suppose I won't?" he said idly.

Von Sternberg never moved and the tension in the atmosphere was like a physical substance.

"You will," Groody told him swiftly, "or we'll hand you over to a few of the Mexicans. Sit down now and say your piece."

"I'd rather stand," Daly told him, his head back and that mask-like face unchanging.

"Sit down," Groody snapped, and his left arm flashed forward. It was half a blow, half a push, and it knocked Daly down into his chair. Groody leaned over him. "Listen.

You haven't got a prayer. You've lost out. I'd hate to do what I may have to do, if the chief'll let me, but by God, I'll do it if you don't talk! Regardless of the chief or anybody else, my neck's valuable to me, understand? Now shoot!"

THERE WAS A long minute's silence. Von Sternberg seemed enthralled by the scene. His lips parted to show his strong white teeth and those long, narrow eyes were unwinking.

"All right," Daly said finally, "God what a rat you are, Groody! If I've got to talk, I prefer to talk to a man that's in the open anyway. Move one side, will you, and let me talk to your master."

Histrionically, the scene was a knockout. The cold contempt in Daly's words was as real as though he meant it. Groody lounged to one side, saying casually, "You can say it to whoever you want to."

There was something more menacing and pregnant with possibilities in Von Sternberg's unbroken silence than there would have been in any exhibition of rage. Evidently, Groody was thinking, he was the kind of man who became more cool and collected and thoughtful in times of stress than under normal conditions. That he could go into temperamental outbursts, he knew, but evidently when a real emergency faced him he had no time for that sort of foolishness.

There was another interval of silence while Von Sternberg and Daly fought a battle with their eyes. Finally Von Sternberg said, "I am waiting."

"There isn't so much too tell, at that," Daly said calmly. "We do know that Dr. Gross is one of your men and we suspect several others in various parts of Mexico. Mr.

Service is down in Mexico City making reasonable headway. To make a long story short, Count, we know nothing very definite aside from your past record but we think that the time has come when you are going to branch out, as it were. Knowledge has been gained of the fact that a considerable part of the Mexican Army in various sections of the country is disaffected. Their generals' loyalty is not unquestioned, I may say, and various signs seem to point to the fact that one of these hardy perennials of a revolution may be just around the corner. That you have an important hand in it, we firmly believe. In fact, I may say that investigations, with the government, the oil companies and others cooperating, we have felt confident would uncover a conspiracy of that sort in more detail within a very short time. I am utterly truthful when I say that up to the present we have nothing too definite, just straws showing which way the wind blows, as it were, but we are boring in plenty."

HE LEANED FORWARD as he took out a cigarette, but his eyes never left Von Sternberg.

"In fact, Count," he said, "powerful as you are, and strong as your position is with a great many Mexicans, including some in high authority, I should advise you to give up all of your plans and to leave the country if you can. Just what your position in this is, I don't know. Naturally, a notorious outlaw, and a German, is never going to be very high in the government. You can claim to have committed your depredations just to get money and resources to help on the revolution, but the most you could be would be a power behind the throne, and stranger things have happened than that those whom you might succeed in helping into power would go back on you when they are in the saddle. It may be that some of these Mexican *jefes* who are conspiring with you merely want the men you can furnish them and, more important, the airplanes. You may think you are the head of it all, and perhaps you are, but taking everything into consideration, I should say you ought to fold your tents and silently steal away."

The Duke was talking quietly, his cultivated voice indicating no emotion, and his words rather more carefully chosen than usual. It was curiously impressive, that repressed monotone, and the very slowness and care with which Daly spoke seemed to make each word hang in the atmosphere as though its significance was immense.

Suddenly Von Sternberg leaned forward, and, as though the spirit within him had been exposed, his whole being seemed to glow with the inner power of the man. Quick questions crackled forth at Daly, and quietly Daly answered them, sometimes with, "I don't know."

Within five minutes, though, the picture had been painted, a picture which did not very closely resemble the actual truth. However, even to Groody it seemed utterly convincing. Von Sternberg had no choice but to believe that his secret organization had been penetrated very deeply; that down in Mexico City the government was starting to prepare for eventualities, and that the loyal sections as well as the prospectively disloyal sections were seething with preparations.

"It looks to me, chief, as though there was only one thing to do," Groody cut in finally, "and that's either to put up or shut up. Are you in shape to get under way immediately? Are preparations thorough enough to have any chance for success if we strike first?"

"We cannot fail," murmured Von Sternberg. "You have done well, Mr. Groody. Johan!"

THAT SHOUT SEEMED to shiver the walls and the little German came running in. There were a dozen orders barked in German and then and there started an afternoon of wild activity.

Daly, under guard of an evil-looking Mexican with a pock-marked face, was secluded in a hut. Groody himself was not asked to do anything. The radio sparked and crackled with messages going out and in, in code. The Cactus Kid, Williams, James and five other pilots, three of them Mexican, flew away from the airdrome and returned one by one with upset Mexicans and one Yaqui Indian. All up and down the valley there was an atmosphere of tenseness and swift planning with a certain deadly undercurrent in it.

Here and there Groody picked up various items of information. One was about special landing fields placed here and there in the monte. Another was a list of close to a dozen sizable towns in which Von Sternberg was king. Third was that someone, apparently an official, but in any event of considerable standing in Mexico City, was second only to Von Sternberg himself as a ringleader in the prospective revolution. Even more than that, Groody picked up the information that messages were leaping back and forth between El Paso and Laredo and Von Sternberg's headquarters. Apparently the Border was honeycombed with Von Sternberg men.

The organization worked with true Prussian efficiency. Planes were being readied and Von Sternberg, sitting in headquarters like a spider in his web, held a constant series of interviews. By nightfall more than a dozen Mexicans of various ranks, most of them generals, were closeted with him.

Landing lights bathed the airdrome, and ships landed and departed as though it were broad daylight.

It was at about this time that Groody decided that he could make a move in the case of Lieutenant Percival Enoch O'Reilly. It was natural that he should be more or less left out of the preparations which were being made, so he had devoted the afternoon to picking up such information as he could. His mind was always busy with what the next move of himself and Daly should be and how it was to be accomplished. They needed to know more, in a way, than they did now, before they were justified in attempting to make a getaway, and O'Reilly was like a weight around his neck.

Twilight had fallen as he made his way casually into the hut where Penoch lay. The Mexican guard greeted him with a respectful smile. In some manner Groody's sardonic sobriquet, "The Black Eagle," had been noised around the camp and the Mexicans looked at him as a sort of a superman. Already they considered him, so he felt, as suddenly having become Von Sternberg's right-hand man.

GROODY GESTURED TOWARD the cot and the Mexican nodded. The two of them went over and looked down at the motionless little figure on the bed. O'Reilly's eyes opened and he stared up at Groody. For a moment Groody's heart seemed to stop beating. There was no madness in those eyes now. In fact they blazed forth at him in complete recognition.

"How do you feel?" Groody asked him, staring down at him as though the very power of his gaze might transfer his thoughts to O'Reilly. The little flyer stared up at him and one eyelid drooped slightly. Then he closed his eyes, mumbled something indistinguishable and turned his head as though in utter weariness. It seemed that he had not comprehended what Groody had said at all.

Groody shrugged his shoulders and gestured to the Mexican, who nodded as though to indicate that it was hopeless to get any sense out of O'Reilly. Groody tapped his head significantly and again the Mexican nodded with a wide grin.

Groody lounged out slowly, but the blood was rushing madly through his body and his mind was very busy.

"That little sucker came to and is stalling," he thought swiftly. "Probably he's heard enough while playing sick to get the hang of the situation someway. Now what to do?"

As he came out the door of the hut he found Wildcat Williams rolling a cigarette.

"Hello," Groody greeted him, and suddenly he wondered whether Williams had been deliberately spying on him. "It looks like a busy day."

"Yeah," said the young Texan, expectorating fluently. "How's your friend O'Reilly?"

"Can't get a word out of him. He's nuts."

Williams' eyes met Groody's and there was no friendship in their depths. A dozen tiny incidents since Groody's arrival with Daly had only cemented the tall flyer's feeling that his standing with Williams and the Cactus Kid was far from high. In a few hours he had apparently usurped the seat at the right hand of the throne and this did not appeal at all to the two outlaws.

"Well, you certainly came in raising plenty of

hell," Williams told him. "Is all this stuff on the level, or is it just some pipe dream?"

"Better ask the chief about that," Groody told him. "It certainly looks on the level to me."

As Williams turned away, the inference in his expression, to say nothing of his words, was plainly that he was not so sure.

Groody had started for the mess hall, his mind busy with a thousand possible plans, when the fat German pilot who had been one of the three whom Groody had captured on the fake holdup came walking rapidly toward him.

"You are wanted at headquarters," he said, "as well as the others."

A LOUD BELL suddenly started clanging furiously from the vicinity of headquarters. From various places men started streaming for headquarters, Mexicans, Germans, one or two Americans, and as far as Groody knew, all of them were pilots.

As he approached headquarters a dozen Mexicans, all talking in voluble excitement and gesturing intensely, came streaming out and down the steps. They gathered at the foot of the steps and the nondescript company of flyers joined them. Groody saw James, his face as pallid and his demeanor as uninterested as ever, and drifted over beside him.

"Hello, old timer. It looks as though things were getting under way," he stated.

"Yes," James said indifferently. "Might as well get it over with, eh, what? You've created a bit of a fuss."

"So it seems. Say, listen, you don't have to answer me if you don't want to. What's the matter with Williams and the Cactus Kid? I seem about as popular as a skunk at a picnic with them."

James' bulging eyes flickered toward Groody and he shrugged his shoulders indifferently.

"Don't mind them. They think they run things. Foolish youngsters, but good men in their place; that is, good for a few things, but without common sense. I'll be glad when it's over. They're not my kind."

He spoke with a sort of weary indifference which indicated that he did not care a great deal one way or the other. Groody wondered considerably about this sandy haired, startlingly pallid Englishman with the dead eyes.

"Probably good family, and has hit the skids, and all that sort of thing," he was thinking.

Wolf came out on the porch and the low drone of excited conversation ceased. Von Sternberg followed them. Outlined in the glow of a single electric light, a chamois jacket over his shirt, and his legs, encased in boots and riding breeches, rather wide apart as though he was bracing himself solidly, the huge German looked down and effortlessly dominated the motley crowd below him. He looked like a veritable Hercules, and now his square face was glowing and the thick blond hair above it caught the light and seemed to be vitalized with the energy within him.

"It has been decided," his resonant bass boomed forth, "tomorrow starts the revolution. All have been notified by radio. To-night we get the extra airplanes. Is Mr. Groody here?"

"Right here," Groody called forth from the gloom.

That wolfish smile played over Von Sternberg's face.

"We go to McMullen and borrow the extra airplanes

which we need," Von Sternberg said. "You will not go along. We have men enough without you and you have done much the last two days. But I know that the long hours would be more pleasant if you know the joke. Not so?"

EVERY EYE WAS on Groody. The Mexican generals were looking at him with admiration and respect. The others, as though his singling out by Von Sternberg had been a mark of special favor, had an air of mingled wonderment and respect.

"Thanks," Groody called back. "But go easy on the boys, will you? Some of 'em are friends of mine. Don't hurt 'em if you can help it."

It was said casually, almost gaily, and Von Sternberg bowed theatrically.

"That will be up to them," he said meticulously. "We have debts to pay the McMullen flight, not so?"

There was a murmur from the other pilots. Two or three times Von Sternberg had found his plans snarled up by Captain Kennard and his merry men.

Suddenly Von Sternberg snapped back into his attitude of crisp domination.

"Our friends will spend the night here and be delivered to their posts tomorrow," he said tersely, gesturing at the group of ornately dressed Mexicans. "You will each get your orders from Johann, individually and immediately. James, you will have the ships ready on the line at ten o'clock. Williams, they will be equipped with double supplies of ammunition. Eight ships, two men to a ship, and relief pilots will fly back the DeHavilands. At 9:30

precisely you will all be here to receive final orders. That is all, gentlemen."

For a moment he stood there as though appraising the men below him. In the wan light of the single electric light globe the scene seemed utterly unreal to Groody's whirling mind. The sombreroed Mexicans, the pilots, almost everyone of whose faces stood out significantly to indicate what manner of men they were, the mountains looming all around them, the mysterious whisper of the monte reaching his ears—it was all like a dream.

Then the real significance of it all swept over him in a wave. Up to McMullen, Slim Evans and Tex McDowell and Sleepy Speers and Captain Kennard were probably in the mess hall. Graves might be there, too. Daly and Penoch under guard, the aerial cavalcade of outlaws about to light the fuse of revolution by raiding the States—

"The next move," Groody thought, "is certainly up to me."

His mind was working like lightning and in the wild excitement generated by anticipation of what was to come and the emergency that faced him, he forgot everything except that the die was cast and that everything rested on his shoulders. For some reason he felt almost like a superman, as though never had he been so physically or mentally capable of doing what had to be done.

His gait was still lounging as he walked toward the mess hall, as though he was relaxing physically for the moment to conserve his energy for the future.

16

IT WAS 9:25 o'clock. On the line before the wide mouth of the cave, eight airplanes were drawn up, gassed and oiled and armed. Already the pilots were gathering at the foot of headquarters steps. The humbler citizens of Von Sternberg's citadel were most of them gathered in a group around the cantina which was in the center of the short street, drinking their beer and talking excitedly. A group of men who acted as mechanics were down near the ships, waiting.

Groody, having drawn an extra Colt from the armory, had two guns on as he walked up the street. He stepped in the hut which had been assigned to him to share with James temporarily, and stole out the back entrance immediately. Half a moment later he was entering the hut where Daly was a prisoner. The Mexican guard was sitting in the doorway, rifle across his knees.

"*Buenos noches, señor,*" said Groody. "How are you feeling, Daly?"

The Mexican smiled ingratiatingly. The word had gone round that Groody was a man to stand in with. He started to rise. Without a split second's warning Groody's fist got the Mexican flush on the jaw and he dropped like a log.

"Quick, Duke!" Groody snapped.

Daly sprang up from the bed where he had been lounging. The Mexican was bound and gagged as Groody told the story in a half a dozen brief sentences.

"I'm not sure of Penoch, but I think so. You can get to his hut without being observed. By going out and through the monte you'll have no trouble. They're too sure of themselves up here. Stay in the bushes alongside the cave at this end until you see me all ready. Then make a break."

ONE MINUTE HAD not elapsed before he was lounging easily out of Daly's hut. The Mexican had been placed under the bed and Daly had gone out the back way. He joined the waiting airmen and the Cactus Kid looked at him and grinned a rather unpleasant grin.

"Funny you're not going along," he drawled. "I didn't suppose we could get along without you now."

"Evidently so," Groody told him.

He was as nervous as a witch and it seemed like an eternity as he waited for any signs of struggle from Penoch's hut. It was the third hut down and his eyes flickered in that direction often.

"How was your friend Daly? I seen you coming out of his shack," the Cactus Kid said in low tones.

"O.K. Thought he might need some cigarettes, or something," Groody told him.

"Yeah? Damned nice of you, I'll say. Maybe he'd like a grand piano, too, to make life more interesting."

Groody had wanted to be at the meeting to discover, if possible, Von Sternberg's exact strategy, but now he realized suddenly that it had been a foolish move. And yet, perhaps not.

He saw James a little distance away from him, uninterested as always. Most of the flyers had their helmets and goggles swinging in their hands and were dressed in coveralls, ready to go. Then, from the mess hall, just as Von Sternberg appeared on the porch, he saw a Mexican emerge with two plates in his hand.

"Good God! Food or something for Daly or Penoch!" Groody thought swiftly.

His mind in a chaos, he drifted back into the darkness. Everybody was looking at Von Sternberg and he was temporarily unobserved, he thought. He slipped around the trees and then walked rapidly down the rear of the huts. Not a sign had come from Penoch's hut, which was on the other side of the street, so Daly had evidently succeeded in getting the guard by surprise. But was Penoch really well enough to leave? At any moment the jig might be up!

HE BROKE INTO a run. He was still unobserved as he got to the end of the street and now he was forced to cross it to go toward the flying field. Trees partially screened headquarters from the street, but just as he gained the other side in safety he heard vague sounds of excitement up above. He ran with long strides through the darkness. Four hundred yards from him were the ships. The landing lights were not on yet and there was no artificial illumination around the cave except for them. He was running through the undergrowth now on the side of the hill as vague shouts came to his ears from up above. Then ahead of him he saw two figures—Penoch and Daly.

"Quick!" he gasped. "Got a gun, Daly? O.K. Penoch, take this one. How do you feel?"

"O.K. Daly's told me the whole works. What's up?"

"They're wise by this time, I'm sure," Groody snapped.

"Duke, swing the prop. I'll get into the cockpit. Penoch, get in the rear. This first Beed."

In an instant they had bounded from cover just as the vanguard of the pursuit cleared the huts six hundred yards away from them. Somebody flung himself on a horse that was in the field and Groody got the impression that it was the Cactus Kid. As they ran forward the mechanics who had been in a group at the lower end of the line started to their feet. For a moment they seemed dazed by what was happening.

"It's O.K., boys, we're just in a hurry," called Groody as he leaped into the cockpit.

In a trice Daly had swung the prop once to suck gas into the cylinders. Groody pushed the selfstarter as Daly came tearing around the ship. Mercifully it worked on the first try. There were three roars from the motor as Groody pushed the throttle to try it out. O'Reilly, his wasted face ablaze, was shooting into the air to hold off the mechanics. Without waiting to warm the motor in the slightest, Groody taxied out, turned the ship southward and the radial motor burst into full cry as the Cactus Kid got within a hundred yards of them. He was shouting something as the Beed went into full career. The landing lights glowed on and the Mexican mechanics were running around like madmen.

Daly was in the back seat with Penoch, and the overloaded Beed took so long a run to get off that it was almost fatal. Groody fairly fought it into the air, its cold motor sputtering occasionally, and it barely cleared the thin fringe of trees on the southern boundary. He throttled the motor then to give it a chance to warm up, and his eyes swept the instruments quickly. Only 65 degrees centigrade was the temperature, and the oil pressure was low, but the motor was working adequately. It would soon be warm.

HE LOOKED AROUND. A stream of pilots were running across the field now. Two ships were already idling and one holding two men started taxying out immediately. That would probably be the Cactus Kid.

Groody circled about, his mind working like lightning. Now the second ship was taxying out, but the other pilots could not possibly take off for three or four minutes.

"My friend the Cactus Kid was right on the job. Maybe suspected something," Groody thought. "Now what to do?"

Should he take off and take a chance on those two chasing him, or should he stop and try to fight them off and waste valuable time which would allow the main body of planes to be only minutes behind him? Daly reached over and gripped his arm. He pointed north. If they stopped now and anything happened, all their work would have been for naught. Groody nodded, pushed the throttle all the way ahead and started climbing to get over the mountains.

Barely five hundred yards behind him the more lightly loaded ship which the Cactus Kid was flying was gaining slowly. It, too, was a Beed, so that they were equal there except for the weight. The two-seated scout, a Falcon, was close behind. Down on the ground the others were taking their time warming their motors.

"They won't figure I can do anything, because even if I get there, I won't be far enough ahead of them to do much good," Groody thought.

Steadily the Beed climbed through the cool night air,

and behind them, moving up slowly but surely, was the other ship. The gauges were reading correctly now and he had no more fears for his motor as the ship hurtled safely across the crest of the mountain and pointed out over the billowing sea of chaparral below.

McMullen was northeast, and he had no fear of the course with the compass in front of him. He would angle toward Tampico, pick up the railroad to Laredo and from it lay a course which would bring him to the Rio Grande not far from McMullen. Every twist and turn in that stream was a guide post to him. It was about three hundred miles, he estimated, and that would be the longest three hours he had ever flown.

Behind him the other Beed came into sight across the mountain top. Barely a thousand feet separated them now and Groody cursed savagely. Maybe the other motor was a little bit more efficient, and the load in his own ship was of course considerably more than the pursuing plane's. Perhaps a thousand yards back of the first Beed was the second ship.

THE MOTOR WAS roaring along wide open at eighteen hundred revolutions a minute and his ship was doing all it could do, and yet, slowly but steadily, the other ship gained.

Groody turned to confront his two companions. Penoch's sunken eyes blazed into his as he gestured back toward the outlaw ship. Daly's handsome face was expressionless, but his eyes, too, were aglow. Groody gestured toward the other Beed significantly. Both of them nodded, standing there side by side in the rear cockpit, and Groody turned his face forward once more. In a moment or two the other ship would be close enough to shoot at them.

It was shooting already. Red dots danced before the muzzles of the front guns, but it was still too far away for accurate marksmanship. Immediately Groody had made up his mind. They were five thousand feet above the chaparral now and a tranquil moon rode high in a velvet sky. It seemed incongruous to associate what was happening with the beauty of the night, and somehow Groody felt as though it could not be true.

Then and there he gambled heavily with Fate. He nosed the Beed down so slightly that the dive was almost undistinguishable. Rapidly it picked up speed—160, 170 miles an hour and finally two hundred as it momentarily left the other ship behind.

He glanced behind him to make certain that the observer's belt was locked around both of the men in the rear cockpit. Again he gestured, and Daly nodded. So abruptly that it seemed almost to twist the sturdy monoplane apart, Groody sent it darting upward as he jammed on right rudder and pulled the stick all the way back in his lap. It flipped over on its back in the twinkling of an eye. For just a second he hung there helpless in the sky, and then the nose came down and it was swooping out, the wires shrilling with the speed and the air speed meter needle up against the peg. It tore downward in a huge arc, three hundred feet below the other ship.

It seemed that the other pilot was taken completely by surprise by that lightning-like maneuver. Groody could see his head thrust over the side of the plane as he searched for him. Groody's ship was hard to see against the dark background of the chaparral.

Then using his excess speed, Groody brought his ship

zooming upward again just as the second Beed went into a frantic bank. He was practically underneath it now. Up and up came the nose until the upper ship crossed the sights. His hand pressed the gun control. He saw his tracers go into the tail. Then one of the greatest combat flyers of the war proceeded to give a lesson in flying.

HIS SHIP HAD almost lost speed in that mighty zoom and was practically standing on its tail, but for two seconds, fighting it with rudder and stick, he kept it there and the nose of his ship followed the tortuous career of the other one as a deadly spray of bullets raked it fore and aft.

Suddenly the nose snapped down in a wing stall. Every last bit of speed had been exhausted. At the same moment the Cactus Kid dived over the side of the upper plane and a parachute whipped out against the night. Groody knew it was he because he passed scarcely a hundred feet to one side of him. He was to know later that the other man in the plane had been Wildcat Williams, and that the corpse of the little outlaw rode the Beed down to the ground and burned in a desert funeral pyre.

Groody's face was grim as he dived his ship like mad to get it out of range of the second bandit plane, now close behind.

"Those two suspicious devils would crab the deal," he thought as the earth lit up in the gigantic flare of the explosion below. "Well, the Cactus Kid will live to tell the tale anyway."

He was now a quarter of a mile in front of the unknown pilot in the second ship but easily a thousand feet lower. In the back seat Daly was crouched down, the double Lewis on its scarf mount pointed back at the pursuer. It was only a matter of seconds before another battle faced them, and this time it would be a desperate one. The other ship had every advantage of position, but it was a Falcon and not quite as maneuverable as a Beed.

Groody had leveled out now and his ship was scooting northward wide open and four thousand feet high.

17

FOR STRAINED, UNENDING minutes the two ships flew along on their respective courses, and still the outlaw ship did not make a move. Because it was so much higher the pilot could have dived at any time and overhauled Groody without trouble. Flying with his head turned, watching the other ship like a hawk, Groody was conscious of mounting surprise at the dilatory tactics of the Falcon. What was his object in delaying his attack, or wasn't he going to attack at all?

Groody's eyes searched the southern sky behind the Falcon and he thought that he could see, ten or perhaps fifteen miles back of it, tiny pin-points of light from the exhausts of the Von Sternberg squadron. Somehow that flight seemed unreal to him as time dragged by without any attack from the leading outlaw.

The night was smooth and cool and now and again white clouds silvered by the moon drifted by placidly. Below the chaparral was like an endless Sea and on each side of the ship the exhaust fires trailed like red banners of defiance. The Falcon was biding its time, but for what? Were other ships to join the Von Sternberg cavalcade at some point further on, or was the Falcon waiting to reach a particular place before going into battle? Somehow that seemed a reasonable assumption to Groody. After all, a ship and pilot could lose a battle without the pilot's being killed, necessarily, and landing in the mesquite so far from civilization wasn't too pleasant a part of the price of defeat.

HE STARTED TO climb very gradually. "Might as well try to pick up a little altitude, if I can," he thought.

Daly leaned over from the back seat.

"We'll watch it," he yelled into Groody's ear. "Why do you suppose he's waiting?"

"Search me," Groody shouted back. He was wondering what desperate strategy he might use when and if that other ship made its attack. There was no "if" about it. Of course, it would, and somehow, some way, he must be out-maneuvered.

At that moment the stakes in the game were secondary to the lanky pilot. In the forefront of his mind were the boys at McMullen, sitting around without the slightest idea that an attack such as had never occurred in the history of the Border patrol was about to be made on them. It would stack up well with the best aerial combats on the Western Front, and to have them caught like rats in a trap was one thing that Groody would not allow if it was humanly possible to stop it. And yet his good common sense told him as the ship flew steadily along through the night that his position was almost a hopeless one.

Any time that that Falcon wanted to go into its dive, the overloaded Beed would be like a crippled duck flapping along in front of the hunter's gun.

"He's waiting for the right spot," he decided.

As though to relax from that desperate strain of endeavoring to find a way out, his mind veered momentarily to O'Reilly. The little flyer was just a shadow of his former self but the tips of his moustache were tilted upward toward the sky again and he was himself mentally at least. What was the explanation of that amazing swoop over the McMullen airdrome, of that wound in his head and of his dramatic appearance above the Von Sternberg airdrome! Groody felt an almost ungovernable impulse to cut the gun and ask him.

Then abruptly he snapped back to himself, and as though the temporary interval in his scheming had rested his mind and made it more efficient, a thought popped into it. He tried to force himself to consider his sudden idea calmly, although every nerve in his body was taut. There were points in its favor. And yet how could it be worked?

His rate of climb had been almost imperceptible. The Falcon had crept closer but Groody had gained four hundred feet and the altimeter stood at forty-four hundred. Far north of him there were three or four points of light, as though from some little village. That might be the spot at which the outlaw would strike.

HE WONDERED WHO it was. He hoped it was one of the Mexicans, most of whom had been taught to fly by Von Sternberg and who probably would not be too expert. He couldn't tell whether there were two men or only one in the other ship, and all the Von Sternberg planes had back seat guns as well as the front ones synchronized to shoot through the propeller. Von Sternberg had used all that he had learned in the German air service to make his aerial army efficient.

Suddenly Groody made up his mind. Better to get it over with than to wait until it suited the other pilot. For a moment more he laid his plans and then in fairness to the others he cut the gun momentarily and shouted his scheme to Daly and O'Reilly. They both nodded.

"Well, I've got one break," Groody reflected grimly, "I could have a half of a lot worse boys along than I've got."

He put the Beed into a steep climb. Far back of them, apparently not gaining an inch, there could be no doubt about the fact that there were little points of light which marked Von Sternberg and his men.

"As a matter of fact they'll have to fly a little slower than we are because some of those ships aren't so fast," Groody thought.

Now as the Beed gained in altitude the Falcon perforce came closer. It was only five hundred yards away now and three hundred feet higher. Groody leveled off and with the throttle all the way on, the Beed picked up speed slowly. Finally he sent it into a very shallow dive until the air speed meter reached two hundred miles an hour. Then he suddenly threw it into a vertical bank. It seemed to turn on a dime and as it straightened out, pointed south, he sent it into a steep dive, losing altitude every moment but gaining speed.

It had darted southward easily three hundred yards before there came a move from the other ship. Groody steepened his dive slightly, flying on a course directly opposite to that of the other ship, and one which would carry him, if the Falcon did not maneuver, directly under his antagonist.

Now came the moment that he had dreaded. The Falcon's nose dipped downward. Again Groody steepened his dive. Could he dart underneath it before it got a shot at him? The Falcon was all the way over in a nose dive.

Groody, with the instinctive forethought which dozens of aerial combats had given him, threw his ship in a vertical bank just in time. Had he continued on his course he would have gone through the barrage which the Falcon laid down. He just escaped it and as the Falcon's pilot seemed to lose sight of him, he banked to the left to get underneath the higher ship, if he could.

THIS TIME HE succeeded. Daly, almost on the floor of the rear cockpit, was shooting directly up at the Falcon. The bandit twisted his ship around as it came level, and was circling above them. Up it went in a wing turn just as Groody zoomed his ship mightily and his front guns got a bead on the plane. A brief burst. He saw his tracers miss it by inches.

The Falcon came sweeping out of its wing turn, but again Groody, four hundred feet lower, banked before it could get a shot at him. It was only a matter of seconds before a good opportunity for the bandit to rake them over would come and he had to throw his ship around like a madman to prevent it. If only that first maneuver had taken the other man by surprise! He must know his onions as a combat flyer, at that, Groody was thinking.

The Falcon was now above him, twisting and turning to follow his own tortuous course, taking an occasional shot at him. Daly, alert as a cat at a rat hole, was sweeping his double Lewis around, but rarely could he get a shot. Each time that Groody, by a quick maneuver, gained two or three seconds' respite from the shooting, he climbed his ship to regain precious altitude. The other pilot, pointed down almost constantly for his shots, was not conserving his own altitude as he should. He was taking six shots to

Groody's one, but slowly the two ships were getting closer to each other as far as altitude was concerned.

Now if Groody could only lead him on and save himself in the process perhaps he could work himself up to a more even position. He dared not consider giving either himself or Daly an opportunity for a good shot except when it came accidentally. It was a game of aerial tag in which he was being chased by an enemy who had the advantage. The most he could hope to do was to stay alive and for the present there was no hope, except by a miracle, of being able to put the other man out of commission.

In order to get a fair shot, the way they were flying, he would have had to expose himself to one which was potentially twice as dangerous. Diving, zooming and banking, two hundred feet below the Falcon which sought to follow him, an eternity of time seemed to pass.

Groody was flying automatically, his eyes never leaving the other ship. Not for a second was the Beed on an even keel. No sooner had the Falcon swept around for a shot than Groody had hurtled his ship out of danger. The Falcon was shooting steadily and the Beed's front and rear guns spoke only occasionally, and meanwhile, creeping up on them, came the hosts of Count Von Sternberg, now but seven or eight miles away.

Suddenly it seemed as though the Falcon's pilot realized that Groody was gradually gaining altitude. For a moment the two ships were flying on a parallel course about three hundred feet apart and with two hundred feet difference in their altitude.

"By God, he's alone as sure as I'm alive!" Groody thought.

HE WAS SLIGHTLY in the rear of the Falcon and just as the bandit ship went into a vertical bank, preparatory to getting straightened away for a shot, Groody zoomed his ship. As his hand pressed the gun control the Falcon seemed to swerve as though the pilot was aware of Groody's intention, and in a swift dive it escaped the burst. Groody could not follow its quick downward course fast enough with the nose of his ship, and a second later the Falcon, now a hundred feet lower, had banked again and was coming head-on, its front guns shooting steadily.

Groody dived steeply to get out of that deadly fire. The motor would protect him, but despite an all-metal prop, any one of those bullets might put the engine out of commission.

He darted underneath the ship at two hundred and fifty miles an hour. As its shadow passed above him he pulled back on the stick. Daly was shooting from the rear seat, but that ultra-skillful pilot above, wise in the ways of combat, banked around in time to escape it. Up and up arched the Beed until it had started on its back as though in a loop. At any second Groody expected that a bullet would burn into him, but one did not come. His ship half on back, he moved rudder and stick with slow sureness. Slowly the Beed came upright, flying on a course directly opposite to the one it had been following when it had gone into the dive and a full five hundred feet higher than it had been.

The windshield shattered before his eyes and splinters flew from the strut to his left. Like a flash he threw it into a vertical bank, searching for the other ship. It was two hundred feet below him and it had been zooming up at his tail before he had banked.

For a moment Daly could not get a shot. The Falcon was

on a blind angle below him. Now the Falcon was directly underneath the Beed and it had lost speed, having stalled at the top of its zoom.

"By God, we've got a chance now!" Groody thought exultantly. "He couldn't get around fast enough to pop us in that Immelmann turn."

The other ship was to the left of him, now four hundred feet below. It came out of the dive which had followed the stall and it, too, arched upward as though to start the same maneuver that Groody had just performed. Like a flash Groody banked and as the Beed darted for that zooming ship he got his guns set. In a second the Falcon would go through his line of fire—

But it did not. The pilot kicked it off in a wing turn. Again Groody passed across it, and now the Falcon was almost as high as he was. The next forty-five seconds was an aerial madhouse. Almost at the same altitude the two ships locked in combat. They went round and round, each one trying to cut across the circle to get a broadside shot at the other one, but each time the destined victim of the maneuver was too smart. It seemed that each man foresaw the moves of the other.

BOTH MOTORS WERE roaring wide open and sometimes above them the *rat-at-tat-tat* of the machine guns was discernible. Wires shrilling and struts vibrating, Groody kept up the fight. His Beed handled a bit logily, due to the weight in the rear seat, but that just about evened things for the extra gun they had.

Suddenly as he found himself in a bank on the opposite side of the circle from the Falcon he almost subconsciously kicked right rudder. The nose flipped downward and to the right. The Beed picked up speed like lightning. As the Falcon turned to meet the challenge, Groody zoomed. Squarely into the nose of the Falcon he sent his shower of bullets. It wouldn't do much good, but it might put him out of commission.

The next second his dazed eyes beheld the Falcon darting by him, and the pilot's two hands were in the air. Daly did not fire. Then the bandit's hands disappeared as his ship fell off into a side slip, and he regained control of it again. He was wide open to a shot now, flying directly away from Groody.

Groody swooped after him and as something familiar struck him about that tall figure in the front seat, he thought, "It's James."

He had reached a point a hundred feet higher than James and barely a hundred feet behind him. He could knock him down easily. James was patting his guns and again his hands went upward in that gesture.

"Jammed," Groody thought.

As though not a moment had intervened between the years of 1917 and '18 and the present, the old creed of the airmen of the Western Front motivated Groody's acts, even his thoughts then. A man with his guns jammed was not shot down. That was sheer murder.

Groody was not conscious of fatigue. Rather it seemed as though a sort of physical and spiritual second wind had come to his aid to make his mind and body work more efficiently than usual. A bizarre idea burst full blown into his mind, loss of an obsession which had had him in its grip for the past few hours. Above all things, McMullen must be warned in time, and now Von Sternberg was less than five miles behind.

Both he and James were flying northward now almost side by side, and with Groody a hundred feet higher. He throttled his ship and put it into a dive as he looked around at Daly and O'Reilly. O'Reilly lifted his arms and shook hands with himself and his mouth opened in some inaudible shout. Daly, cool and, collected, nevertheless seemed to be warmed by an inward glow. Groody cut the gun all the way as his ship dived down toward James.

"He's out of commission," he yelled. "I've got a little scheme. See how close those boys are back there? We can't beat 'em into McMullen by five minutes, and they know it."

AS HE CAME closer to James he wondered whether Von Sternberg had picked them up. The periodic clouds through, under and over which they had passed at various times, might just possibly have prevented the oncoming flyers from seeing too much of what had happened. There was one wreck back along the trail which they couldn't have missed. It was just possible that Von Sternberg might think that it was Groody.

"No, that isn't possible," he thought, "because his own men would have come back and joined him if everything had been O.K. God, I wonder if we can get away with this?"

He was almost alongside James now and there was no other outlaw in Von Sternberg's organization except possibly the chief himself, with whom he would have considered taking the risk, which, in his present state of transcendent mental clarity and recklessness, he was going to take now.

He took out his handkerchief—the two ships barely fifty feet apart—waved it and pointed to the motionless James.

He was trying to get James' word that he had surrendered. A little more sign language, and James suddenly waved a handkerchief, or something white, back at Groody, after patting his guns significantly. He had surrendered.

Groody saw that there were back seat guns, which, due to the fact that James was alone in his ship, had been useless to him. Then Groody cut the gun of the Beed again and motioned O'Reilly and Daly to lean over close to him. He shouted his scheme into their ears. He was called assorted varieties of a damn fool, but finally he won his point.

Ahead of them loomed a huge silver mound of mist easily a quarter of a mile wide and a thousand feet high. Groody directed James to fly around it to the left and with his own ship flying formation so close that he could actually see the Englishman's eyes, he followed him.

Von Sternberg and his men were out of sight temporarily, behind some other clouds. No sooner had they started to skirt the cloud than it seemed as though the ship picked up tremendous speed. The mist, within twenty feet of his wing tip, was like a solid substance. One hundred and fifty miles an hour which had seemed to be barely crawling across the earth below was a truly dizzying speed in reference to the cloud.

Now, Groody's hawk-like face seemed to lose its sardonic quality and to become curiously boyish as he used the sign language again. He pointed to himself, then to the upper wing, then to James and with his two hands went into still further detail of what he wanted done. It took a full minute for James to comprehend, even if he did then, but finally it seemed that he did.

GROODY MOTIONED TO Daly. Daly unloosened his belt

and climbed forward into the front cockpit. Groody was standing up, flying with one hand, and without the use of the rudder. As Daly slipped into the seat his eyes glowed warmly into Groody's.

"With you it's probably all right," he yelled, "and by God it may solve the problem, if I can pick up landmarks enough to find my way. By God, I can! The Penuco!"

He shouted a few more words and Groody nodded. He was like some devil of the upper air concocting mischief and enjoying it thoroughly. A moment later, standing on the seat alongside Daly and holding to the upper wing, his head thrust itself up into the terrific air blast. No one of the three of them had parachutes, although James did have.

Many hours of stunt work with his own flying circus and as a stunt man in Hollywood made the first part of his task comparatively easy to him.

Leaning against the terrific air stream, he got to his knees on the upper wing and crawled to the front of it. His hands over the leading edge of the wing, he snaked his way to the tip as Daly's practiced hands took over the ship and kept it level despite his weight. Almost at the extreme tip he gripped the cabane strut set there for the aileron controls and got to his knees as he gripped it.

James had dropped back temporarily, and now as Daly throttled slightly James started moving up. Crouched there a mile above the earth, Groody's heart for a moment failed him. That was a bandit back there and one of a peculiar breed. He was utterly at James' mercy, and yet, somehow he felt that James would live up to his creed. Did he not have the word of the man who, back close to Querrara, had seemed to expect his word to be taken as one gentleman's to another? In any event it had to be done. McMullen was coming closer with every moment and somehow it seemed to Groody that the fate of the world itself depended on the successful culmination of his plan at that moment.

He was on his right knee, his left foot on the wing, and one hand gripping that strut as James, slightly to the left of the Beed, and ten or fifteen feet higher, crept closer. Groody was staring almost squarely into the circle of light which represented the propeller as James' right wing crept up the fuselage of the Beed.

JAMES COULDN'T BE a traitor right then, Groody thought. He was utterly helpless, with his guns jammed, and Penoch O'Reilly had the rear seat Lewis trained squarely on the Englishman as though to keep the outlaw's mind on his work. And what a flyer James was!

Now Groody was squatting on his heels, his body inclined forward to compensate for the air stream which seemed bent on tearing him off. He did not look down from his frail perch. The thing which had made it possible for him to be a stunt man was more important than the stringy steel muscles in his lanky body. It was a power of ferocious concentration which would enable him to consider walking a six inch pathway five thousand feet in the air as though it was on the ground, and so now his world was crystallized in the wing skid coming toward him.

He came almost upright, body leaning at an angle of almost forty-five degrees. His hand had left the cabane strut and he was balancing almost on the wing tip, his eyes never leaving the wing skid three feet behind him and probably four feet higher than he was.

Penoch, in the rear seat, was motioning to James. Daly's face was like a white blotch in the darkness. Now the wing skid was almost directly over him, but too high to reach even if he straightened to his full length.

Then and there the right wing of the Falcon seemed to fairly swoop down at him. James had banked slightly and Groody had to duck slightly to escape being hit on the head. His left elbow dug itself into the wing skid, like a hook into an eyelet. Again Penoch signaled and the Falcon seemed to leap ahead, its new burden swinging beneath it.

Groody's right hand was gripping his left one. Now, the shock of the transfer over, his right hand found the wing skid and for a second he hung by it alone as his body swayed in the air stream and his left hand groped for the opening on the wing tip, there to give a mechanic a grip in swinging the ship on the ground.

He got his hold and this time his weight was supported by the left hand alone as he groped for the strut with his right one. He found it, and slowly, like a man chinning himself, he dragged himself up until his head was above the wing and he was staring into the begoggled eyes of James, fifteen feet away from him.

It was the work of but a minute for Groody to draw himself up and he subsided on the wing tip in sudden complete exhaustion. His heart was pounding and his mouth was dry, but there he was.

18

THE BEED WAS now slightly back of the Falcon and Penoch's ever-ready gun was still trained on them. For a moment Groody remained on the wing in utter relaxation. He saw James lift his hand as though in salute to him, but he scarcely noticed it. Incongruously enough as he thought of the future it seemed as though everything came to him at once, and that all the details from Mexico City to McMullen were crystal clear.

Service would have notified the government and over night, while the Mexican generals were still at Von Sternberg's headquarters, preparations would be under way to scotch the impending revolution. Tampico would have been notified surely by morning. The authorities would be ready to throttle the widely laid plans before they had fairly gotten under way. Really all that was left as his responsibility was the round up of the Von Sternberg gang, and that should happen at McMullen.

Slowly he began to inch his way along the wing. As he reached the front cockpit he did not immediately start to make his way into the rear seat. He stared into the bulging eyes of the pallid Englishman and, as he did so, a sort of wintry smile appeared below James' closely clipped mustache and for just a moment those cold eyes seemed to lighten.

GROODY REACHED OVER and cut the throttle. For the first time in several minutes he really remembered the Von Sternberg squadron and glanced behind him. That huge cloud hid them still.

"Thanks," he yelled. "Now you can do one of two things." He had on a gun but he did not draw it. A quick look showed him that James had two Colts on his hip, but with the Beed so close surely he would not attempt to use them even were it in his mind. "You can give me your word that you'll be nothing but a passenger, not making one move, or you can jump in your chute right now."

James leaned forward.

"I'm your prisoner," he declared. "I give my word not to try to escape."

"All right. Take off your guns and then let me get into this front cockpit, and you get into the rear."

James removed the guns and placed them on the floor of the cockpit and then stood up. Groody tumbled into the cockpit and took over the stick. The Falcon bucked and skidded as James silently climbed into the rear seat.

"I think his word's good," Groody thought to himself, slightly troubled, as the ship steadily made its way northward, "but I can't take any chances now."

Quick orders were given to James and in obedience to them he stood up with his back toward Groody. With the stick between his knees, Groody used his necktie to bind the outlaw's hands behind him. He didn't want a wrench caressing his head at an important moment.

He set the adjustable stabilizer and left the ship to its own devices for a moment as he clasped the observer's belt around the helpless James. Another order was given the Englishman and James shrugged his shoulders.

"I can do nothing else," he yelled into Groody's ear, "and I gave you my word. I want you to know this, though. If I did not know you could throw me overboard and do it anyway, I should never have given my word. Had I known it a few moments ago—"

"That's ancient history," bawled Groody. "All right, lean way forward here so we can make the switch."

James had on extraordinarily large square goggles and a close fitting, soft helmet very similar to Groody's own. He also had on a tightly knotted bandanna around his neck and his shirt was open. The bandanna was evidently a sort of wind breaker. In a few seconds, Groody had turned himself into as close a replica of James as was possible under the circumstances by putting on his goggles and bandanna.

AT ANY MOMENT Von Sternberg's men might come into sight, although there were numerous small clouds drifting across the path of the two ships. Groody knew that there were various specially constructed flying fields here and there and that some of Von Sternberg's ships could not carry gas enough to reach McMullen in one hop. There would be a landing somewhere, probably, which might complicate matters.

He was thinking of this and a thousand other things as he busied himself investigating James' front guns. Naturally James had had no opportunity to fix up a jam in the middle of that titanic battle.

Groody's lean face split into a wide grin as his practiced fingers and eyes discovered the fact that the jam was a simple one. One of the cartridges had simply stuck. It did not take him two minutes to adjust it and get the ammunition belt working smoothly again. He tried out his guns twice and they worked perfectly.

He throttled his motor and eased over toward the Beed. He signaled that all was well, and just at that moment, like a good omen, a wide silver ribbon came into view as they burst through a wisp of cloud. Several hundred yards wide, flowing in stately majesty through the jungle, it could be nothing but the Panuco.

He signaled to Daly and Daly nodded. Along the banks of that river there was a big oil development somewhere. Daly could find that much more quickly than they could reach McMullen. There would be a private oil company telephone wire there and it should not take very long to get into communication with the Border. It was just an additional factor of safety, and part of that horrible feeling that a motor cutting out or the slightest accident of any kind happening would result in a tragedy and McMullen would be gone.

Two minutes later, the clouds less thick now, Daly was flying eastward down the river in search of civilization. If necessary, Daly could go all the way to Tampico and reach there much more quickly than he could reach McMullen.

Less than five minutes later, though, the run of luck which had come their way exhausted itself. Just as Von Sternberg's men came in sight, now almost ten miles back of them, Groody saw Daly spiraling down toward a clearing on the edge of the lordly stream. He did not dare fly over there, but his heart in his mouth, he saw them land safely. Something had gone wrong. Possibly the radiator had sprung a leak or something equally minor had happened, but completely invalidated their plans.

GROODY SWUNG HIS ship around and it swept in wide circles as he watched the on-coming Von Sternberg. It was almost a miracle that Daly and O'Reilly had landed safely in the wan moonlight in a strange field, but that was the only bright spot in the situation. There was one thing certain, however. The boys at McMullen would be knocked off like rats in a trap unless something happened to save them, and this something, would have to be through the exclusive instrumentality of Mr. George Groody.

Right then it seemed that the reaction from days of solid strain and almost unending physical effort set in in all its force. For a moment Groody felt that the weight of the world was on his shoulders and that he could not bear up under it. All by himself, worried sick, the fate of a dozen of his oldest friends in the balance, one hundred and fifty miles out over the monte at midnight with his enemies roaring toward him—the future seemed like a blank wall in which there was no opening.

He shook himself wearily and suddenly sat bolt upright as though the physical gesture would have a mental effect. He fairly whipped his mind into action. Then, because of the kind of man he was, what seemed like insuperable odds suddenly became a challenge flung at him.

There was so little hope that a curious fatalism swept over him. His face became more saturnine than usual and as a sudden freakish idea popped into his head his mouth widened in that one-sided smile.

As he spiraled his ship higher and higher to reach the level of the on-coming Von Sternberg planes, he searched in the tool kit. He found some tape and quickly tore a small piece into a triangular shape. This he pasted on his upper lip, grinning at the conceit, in what might pass from a distance as an imitation of James' mustache. He turned around and motioned to James, and that lanky gentleman obediently slouched out of sight.

His face grim and set, but all his characteristic mockery observable in it, his sloping eyes glinting behind those huge square goggles, he flew to meet his enemies. All he could do was shoot the works, and he wished with all his heart that he had a cigar to help him through the ordeal.

19

HE RECOGNIZED VON Sternberg's private monoplane, also a Beed, leading the loose formation. Taking care to keep a hundred and fifty feet away so that his face would be almost indistinguishable in the darkness, he signaled that all was well. His hand gestured twice, indicating a tail spin, and he sought to convey the information that he, James, had knocked down the fleeing ship and that the Cactus Kid and Williams had also fallen by the wayside.

The huge figure of Von Sternberg was motionless in the cockpit of his ship as Groody flew alongside him, but finally his hand raised in a salute.

"He understands and he believes I'm James," Groody thought to himself.

Gradually he slipped back until he was in the rear of the loose formation of six planes. Well, he had expected to get away that far. After all, anyone would recognize the fact that it was James' ship and no one could conceivably suspect that anything was wrong unless they actually saw that it was Groody who was flying it.

"That Britisher could certainly have done me dirt," Groody reflected, but somehow he had no real fear of James being untrue to his word.

THE FORMATION ROARED steadily northward and Groody saw that Von Sternberg was still climbing, but very gradually. They were ten thousand feet high now and the cool air began to go through Groody like a knife. It would not be long now, and what on earth was he to do when the emergency came?

Fifty miles north of the Panuco and only a hundred miles from the Border, and there was still no evidence that the formation was going to land anywhere. Somehow, without knowing definitely just why, Groody had sort of counted on that, and yet he was aware of the fact that any move he might make out here over the monte, such as destroying the ships of the formation after they had reached the ground to re-gas, would be in a sense abortive. It might save McMullen a lot of grief, but Von Sternberg would not be captured. Of course he could be killed in cold blood, and yet Groody shrank from that. He could pounce on him now and knock him down, and take his chances thereafter, but it didn't seem to be cricket to the rangy flyer. Furthermore, Von Sternberg was far more valuable alive than dead. This should be a real round-up and the Von Sternberg menace should be scotched completely.

Then suddenly a thought came to him.

"That's the reason they took so long catching up to us," he thought. "They landed to re-gas back there."

He cut the motor momentarily, being a safe fifty yards behind the last ship and allowed James to come in sight again to rest his muscles.

"Don't hesitate too long when I tell you to pop down again, though," he yelled, and the impassive Englishman nodded.

As they flew along toward the Border, Groody's mind was working along methodically. It was just like Von Sternberg to make this gesture a few hours before the revolution broke—to have his little fling at the United States, to pay off his debts to the McMullen flight, to use their ships to help on his plan—it was a perfect layout for the ego-maniac. Laredo would have been almost seventy-five miles nearer for airplanes than McMullen, but what was seventy-five miles to Von Sternberg after he had built up a dramatic coup in his own mind?

Groody wondered about the flyers in that aerial cavalcade. Wolf was probably an excellent pilot. That fat little German who had been James' companion during the fake hold-up looked as though he might be a war veteran, as well. But the others, he believed, must be more or less newly trained Mexicans whose flying ability was not too great. As a matter of fact, that formation didn't show the automatic skill of veteran flyers. He believed that in James, the Cactus Kid and Williams he had already disposed of three of the aces of Von Sternberg's flying organization.

"The Count himself, Wolf, and the other Dutchman," he thought. "That's three good flyers. The other three probably don't amount to much."

SOMEHOW IT WAS a shock to him to see the Rio Grande come in sight. Far to the east there was a splotch of light against the sky. That would be McMullen unless his eyes deceived him. Then as he saw a big bend in the river, he knew that it was McMullen.

He drew himself together and came out of the semi-trance which had had him in its grip during that long hour and a quarter in which he had been following the Von Sternberg planes. Thirteen thousand feet high, they were, and within eight or ten minutes they'd be over McMullen.

Von Sternberg had angled across the chaparral, bound squarely for the town. Groody looked at his watch. One o'clock in the morning. Perhaps the bridge foursome—Captain Kennard, Beaman, George Hickman and Sleepy Speers, was still engaged in their nightly battle, and maybe Slim and Tex and three or four of the others were still raising and re-raising each other in the recreation room to the music of clinking chips. Perhaps someone along the river would telephone the news of that aerial cavalcade, and yet it was so high in the night sky that perhaps the drone of it, and its practical invisibility, would result in no one noticing it.

Groody shoved the throttle all the way on and started climbing steeply. No one was noticing him, so far as he knew, and he had dropped one hundred yards back of the formation. He maintained that distance, and his wide open motor enabled him to climb without losing ground. He could not do anything yet. He had no hope of eventually winning any battle, and he would simply be finally knocked down into the monte with McMullen still unwarned. That fatalism still possessed him, and somehow it drove out all thought of fear. His back was squarely against the wall and what would happen, would happen.

Now they were over the river and ahead of him Von Sternberg started into a power dive. Obediently the other ships followed him as the speed picked up terrifically and they swooped down to pounce on their prey. Five miles ahead, like a white pocket handkerchief in the mesquite, was the McMullen airdrome. The lights on the hangars which bounded it to east and west outlined it like so many fireflies, and the white row of buildings on the southern end seemed like an intermittent fence.

Nine thousand feet high, three miles away, and now he knew that the accustomed ears of the McMullen men would have caught the earth-shaking roar of that gliding squadron.

Groody took a long breath, and from his post one thousand feet higher than the others, he nosed over into practically a nose dive. He swooped down on the last ship like a hawk on its prey. Three hundred feet from it, and he pressed his gun control. His bullets poured into it in a deadly shower. The ship faltered and started spinning downward.

"And, by God, nobody knows it!" Groody thought to himself.

HE TURNED HIS attention to the next one in line, the position of which had been fifty feet ahead of his victim and a hundred feet to one side. Concentrated on that airdrome ahead and on handling their ships in that dive, not a pilot in the crew knew that one of their comrades was down.

The air speed meter needle was up against the peg and the Falcon was hurtling itself through the air like a cannon ball. Again Groody's guns spoke just as the landing lights of the McMullen airdrome flooded on and wildly rushing figures could be seen streaking across its surface.

Three short bursts and another Von Sternberg ship went dipping and fluttering downward and one parachute whipped out whitely against the dark of the earth. The man who had been flying almost alongside of the victim looked around in startled comprehension, but it was too late. Just as he banked his ship, Groody, so close to him that he could see both passengers' mouths open as though in shouts of anguished fear, poured his hail of lead into them.

Three ships were down and now they were but a thousand feet high and barely a thousand yards back of the airdrome. The wires of the Falcon were screaming with the speed and the motor seemed about to jump from its bed, as Groody remorselessly kept the throttle all the way ahead.

A hundred yards ahead of him, two ships, probably flown by the two Germans, which had been following Von Sternberg closely, abruptly banked to the right and left. Groody used his terrific speed to zoom upward, and gain four hundred feet.

The McMullen airdrome was a madhouse. The one ship on the line for emergency duty had its propeller going and two men were flinging themselves into it.

Von Sternberg in the lead had never faltered in his course. His Beed was going like a rocket, pointed straight for that ship. He was evidently unaware of what had happened behind him, or if he was, he did not let it shake him.

Below Groody, the two ships which were aware of his intentions had now turned, prepared to give battle. He was four hundred feet higher and at once he had made up his mind. As though completely forgetful of his other two antagonists, he jammed the stick all the way ahead, and in practically a full nose dive, sent his shivering and shaking plane straight toward the ground.

Von Sternberg was coming down at an angle, swooping across the buildings on the southern edge of the field.

"He can mow down everybody in that airdrome all

by himself!" was the wild thought which shot through Groody's numbed brain.

HE HIMSELF DID not dare to shoot yet as he darted down at Von Sternberg. He was scarcely aware of a hail of bullets which got the fuselage of his ship from the left hand bandit plane. His mind was concentrated on the plane below.

A cloud of dust sprang up twenty-five feet from the DeHaviland which was taxying out on the field, and at that moment Groody's own guns spoke. His tracers went through the left wing of the Beed below, but before he could get his madly diving ship straightened out for a better shot, Von Sternberg zoomed mightily. Those bullet holes in his wing had made him aware of what was happening and for a moment he forgot his prospective victim below in favor of the menace in the air.

"Probably surprised him a little," Groody thought grimly as with both hands he strove to get his ship out of that terrific dive.

He made it, barely a hundred feet above the ground and for a moment he had a horrible feeling that his elevators or wings would snap off under the terrific strain.

Von Sternberg was turning high above him for a shot, and behind him the other two ships were diving at him. Up and up went the Falcon, twisting slightly on its course to spoil the aim of the others as three more DeHavilands came trundling out of the hangars below.

Twelve hundred feet high now and Groody was flying almost without conscious thought. He was twisting and turning his ship without rhyme or reason. In that aerial madhouse he merely strove for the moment to save himself.

A ship loomed before him and he shot automatically at

it, but missed it. The air seemed full of roaring airplanes. Then as he turned his ship in a vertical bank he saw one of the bandit planes swooping down again at the ground. Ahead of him, just wing-turning for another shot was Von Sternberg. At one side a second ship was zooming at him. Again Groody dived his Falcon at the ship which was swooping down at the hangar, firing as it went. Careless of the other two, Groody got his bead on the plane he was attacking.

He kept the gun control down for a full three seconds, his steady hand on the stick, changing the course of the plane almost infinitesimally, to follow the other ship. It burst into flame a hundred feet above the ground and fell between two of the hangars.

A sensation as though a red-hot poker had been thrust through the back of his neck stunned him for a second. There were bullet holes all through his ship as he banked barely seventy-five feet above the ground and shot across the airdrome.

Both German ships were diving at him now and for one wild second he knew that he was looking squarely into the jaws of death.

It was there that the miracle happened. He could scarcely believe his eyes, and his dazed mind could not comprehend its significance just then, but rocketing down out of the sky came another ship, a Beed.

He saw the bandit plane to his right come up and stall and fall off on a wing, as that new plane poured its hail of lead into it.

"Daly and Penoch, by God!" Groody shouted to himself.

His back was wet with blood and at that second another bullet got him in the leg.

THEN THERE CAME a moment's respite. His Falcon shot upward over the hangars on the western side of the field and Von Sternberg, who had been diving at him, turned to meet the attack of the other plane.

Groody tried to turn his plane to join in the battle. Then he looked down stupidly. He could not move his left leg. A great wave of weakness swept over him. Suddenly he was fighting for consciousness as he slowly and painfully turned his plane around for a landing. The world was like a reeling dream as the Falcon staggered northward and turned in for the landing.

The two Beeds over the airdrome were fighting their battle scarcely five hundred feet high, but they seemed to be in another world as far as Groody was concerned. He watched three DeHavilands take off and his mind could not exactly grasp the reason for it.

The two Beeds, their lack of altitude preventing the ordinary maneuvers, seemed to be like two ground animals locked in combat, banking and turning almost on each other's tails, as Von Sternberg fought for his life. In a quick turn he took time for one pot shot at a rising D.H. and the ship went down like a shot. Somehow that temporarily brought the half conscious Groody to.

"What a man!" he thought dazedly, and at that moment his wheels hit the ground. The ship bounded mightily and then looming before his eyes was another DeHaviland taxying out on the field. With his last conscious thought he jammed right rudder on and turned the Falcon sharply to avoid a collision.

His right wing dipped into the ground, its nose came down and as the tail flipped around through the air, Groody slipped off into unconsciousness.

20

HE CAME TO himself staring up at familiar brown canvas. He was on a cot in a tent and sitting over against the wall, calmly looking over a newspaper, was the weazened figure of Major Searles, the flight surgeon.

Groody felt very weak, but otherwise well, and he noticed that the Major's sartorial custom of winding four or five stocks around his thin neck to make the collar of his uniform fit had not been changed for the occasion. He did not speak for a minute as he reconstructed what had happened. There was a bandage around his neck and his leg felt funny, and he wondered how important those wounds were going to be, without seeming to take particular interest in them. Then he became aware of the fact that his left arm was bandaged, including the hand, almost to the shoulder, and that it was very uncomfortable. Now that he thought of it, he had a bandage around his head and cheek as well.

"Strikes me as though I'm somewhat of a cripple," he thought. Then he said aloud, "Well, Major, what's the latest news?"

The Major dropped his paper as though he had been shot.

THERE WERE VOICES coming from without, and Groody could hear Slim Evans stating as he came down the boardwalk, "That's what I call a scrap, you little devil, you. I wonder if Groody's O.K. by now?"

"How do you feel?" Major Searles asked, coming pattering over to the bedside like a chipper little sparrow. His kind old eyes shone through his nose glasses as he automatically felt Groody's face.

"Not so bad. What happened to Von Sternberg?"

"We've got him, and he hasn't got a scratch on him. Daly and O'Reilly knocked him down."

"Well, then, what happened to me?" Groody inquired.

"Well, we took a bullet out of your left leg—it's been two hours since you went under. That's just a flesh wound in the neck, and the bullet in your thigh fortunately didn't get a bone."

"What's all these bandages?"

"Your ship caught fire and before James could get you out you got burned a little. Nothing serious, though."

"James got me out, huh?"

"Yes. Burned himself pretty bad doing it, too. He's in the hospital in McMullen. He'll come around all right. Nervy chap."

A head peeked through the tent flap and the elongated figure of Lieutenant Slimuel X. Evans entered, followed in file by Lieutenant Penoch O'Reilly.

"Greetings and salutations," Slim said cheerily. "Shame you weren't killed to put you out of your misery. How do you feel?"

"Oke," answered Groody. "You couldn't rustle a cigar around this camp, could you?"

"I shall try and quickly," responded Evans and disappeared.

O'Reilly strode forward twirling his little mustache in a highly chipper and self-satisfied manner.

"Some night," he boomed in that deep bass. "Little tourist flight from Mexico, eh? Ho! Ho! Ho!"

"Yeah," nodded Groody. Somehow it was infinitely pleasant to have the strain over and for the moment his wounds seemed a blessing rather than a curse. They would give him a good excuse to lay around and be helpless. "By the way, I never have gotten the straight of what happened to you."

"Now, don't talk too much," warned the doctor. "You're not so strong, you know. You lost a lot of blood."

"That's all right. I've got nothing to do but rest from now on," Groody informed him. "How come your galavanting around Mexico for so long and thumbing your nose at us here at McMullen that night?"

O'REILLY PLANTED HIMSELF on widely separated legs as though prepared to defend himself against the world and his eyes glowed forth at Groody.

"Believe it or not, I can't remember one damn thing from the time that I had a battle in the air with a guy that captured me and put me in that ship they tell me I later flew over the airdrome here.

"I was coming up the Border from Laredo and there was a ship on the ground and the pilot was waving at me. When I landed another guy leaps out of the bushes, and they proved to be none other than a couple of our old friend Von Sternberg's men. How he got wise to when my patrol was, I don't know, or maybe they didn't care whether it was me or not. They just wanted a ship. Going to play a little trick on the patrol.

"Anyway, one guy takes my ship with Gravesend in it, and the other fellow has me tied up in his own. That was the Beed. What happened to the D.H. I don't know. I guess Gravesend tried to pull the same stunt I did and they ended up in that wreck. Anyway, I got loose from the bonds and lit into this other guy and tried to take him. He hit me a lick, or maybe several of them, around the head, gave me concussion of the brain, or something, the doctor thinks, and I sort of went out like a light—not unconscious, but loony.

"Well, you certainly were up to a lot of tricks for a maniac," Groody informed him.

"He just had had Von Sternberg on his mind so much," Major Searles cut in, "and it was such a mania with him, that he automatically started out to get him in his own fanatical way."

"I must have flown over the airdrome here to show you all that I was all right," O'Reilly said. "Damn considerate of me, what? Ho! Ho! Ho!"

"Well, how did you ever get to Von Sternberg's place?"

"Oh, I was landing around Mexico, begging food, raising hell generally, and I've got a vague recollection of knocking the truth out of some Mexican about fifty or sixty miles away from Von Sternberg's place. Had a hell of a time getting gas everywhere too, I seem to remember. But, so help me, when I came to myself I had no idea where I was. I had to overhear a lot of talk to get wise to myself, and then I played sick until I could figure out some way of getting out of there. I was going to shoot Von Sternberg if it was the last thing I did.

"The first time I heard your name in conversation,

George, I sort of got the hang of it. I'd heard you were a fast worker, but when I found out you were right among 'em, I said to myself, says I, 'I'll bet George and I are going to get away with this,' so I laid there, never said a word and pretended to be a cross between unconscious and nuts. Had a lot of fun. Ho! Ho! Ho!"

THAT RABELAISIAN LAUGH reverberated from the tent and caused Slim Evans, who entered at the head of a procession composed of the Federal Secret Service officers, Graves, Daly and Captain Kennard, to say: "If you'd laughed when you were sick down there, we'd have all known where you were and could have dropped in and picked you up. Here's your rope, Groody."

"Hello, Duke. Hi, Captain. Hello, Mr. Graves," Groody said casually. He lit the cigar and drew in a slow, satisfied puff as Graves came to the side of his bed. His remarkable eyes were shining warmly.

"Good night's work, Groody," he said quietly, "and you will not regret it."

"Well, I'm glad it's over," Groody informed him. "These things are a hell of a lot nicer to talk about than they are to go through, but I had some fun, at that. How do you feel Duke? Boy, when you landed down there I thought the jig was up."

"Clogged jets," Daly said quietly.

"Well, how is everything along the Potomac?" Groody inquired, the cigar so far in one corner of his mouth that that one-sided line was etched very deeply in his leathery cheek. "What became of those boys that I bumped off on the way in here?"

"Two of 'em's dead, and the rest of 'em more or less crippled, and we've got 'em all rounded up and in the hospital," Kennard said raucously. "Our friend the Count they've got over in Tent 6 guarded by everybody except the Chink. Hasn't got a scratch and just grins and kids us."

"I'd like to see him," Groody said.

"Well, I guess we can do that for a sick man," Kennard informed him. "Penoch, hop over and tell about six of the guards to escort your boy-friend over here, will you. Then you might tell the Chink to make up some coffee. No sense in going to bed now."

"What about things down in Mexico? I suppose Mexico City knows all about it?"

"Of course," Graves slid in evenly, "I've been on the telephone for almost a solid two hours. By noon to-morrow those Mexican generals will be in custody and there is no question that the entire movement will have been stopped and that the general public will doubtless know nothing about it. Information has been coming in rapidly, so I am told, for the last twenty-four hours on the leads supplied by you gentlemen, and the disaffected territory is known almost exactly. There is no question that a great majority of the ringleaders will be apprehended in a few hours. Eight planes are leaving Mexico City at dawn for Von Starnberg's headquarters, which, of course, is somewhat out of the province of the United States of America, but which, I am sure, the government will approve. In any event, your particular job, the breaking of Von Sternberg, has been accomplished."

"Thanks to Groody mainly," Daly said evenly.

"Thanks to nobody in particular," Groody informed him. "I didn't see anybody doing any shirking."

His eyes lingered for a moment on that handsome, startlingly boyish face before him with the eyes of an old man. The shadow in them had temporarily lifted, it seemed.

"His face lies and his eyes don't," Groody thought. "He's like a banty rooster with the power to change himself into an eagle. I'd sort of like to know that hombre better, but I'll bet it would be a tough job to get under that shell of his."

There were footsteps outside and a moment later the huge figure of Von Sternberg filled the tent opening, followed by two guards. He clicked his heels together and bowed, showing his teeth in the smile which had become so familiar to Groody.

"You are feeling better, I trust?" he said carefully.

"Better than I have in a long while. Well, Count, I just wanted to see you and tell you there's no hard feelings before they ship me to the hospital, as I suppose they will. I was sorry to have to lie to you so much, but you know how it is."

Von Sternberg bowed again. He shrugged his shoulders and lit a cigarette with elaborate nonchalance. He was playing his part to the hilt, but somehow Groody sensed what a raging chaos of emotion lay below his contained exterior.

"It's of no importance," Von Sternberg said easily, "and there will come a day—"

Suddenly Groody was aware of a wave of weakness. He felt himself sinking uncontrollably into slumber.

"Well," he said drowsily, a hint of the old sardonic smile on his face, "give me a break, will you? Don't let it come until I have my health."

Whereupon, without any further ceremony whatsoever, he went to sleep.